The Co

CW01464777

TG Trouper

Contact: tgtrouper@gmail.com

Acknowledgements

I wish to thank my wife for putting up with my silences, blank stares and mutterings while I write my books. I also thank my sister Pam and my friends Sally, Julia, Gary, Dave and Baz for their continued support and encouragement.

I am eternally grateful to all those who have purchased and enjoyed my works, particularly those who message me and say as much. Thank you, it makes a big difference.

Dedication

No AI was used it the writing of this novel and as such it is dedicated to all those other authors who retain their integrity by refusing to use AI to write their novels for them.

The clue is in the name 'artificial'. People want to read stories from the human mind, not something that has been cobbled together in a microsecond by copying works from other authors.

When purchasing a book, readers should ask if any AI has been used to write the book, and if any part of the work has been artificially generated then the reader should refuse to buy it.

The Collaborator

Introduction

The city state of Matrea was founded over two thousand years ago. For five hundred years it grew in size and power, becoming a sophisticated democracy. Its inhabitants were citizens, subject to no single leader, only to the law. Culture emerged, and the people enjoyed freedom and liberty. Matrean ideas and influence began to spread. At the turn of the sixth century the Matrean ideal had spread across the globe. The world entered a period of stability that was to last for another five hundred years.

Then the Calder dynasty came to power and systematically reversed all of the freedoms that the citizens had enjoyed.

In the year 1027 a secret organisation emerged. It was called the 1027 Committee and dedicated itself to the overthrow of the Calder bloodline. For a thousand years they have tried but have always failed. With each attempt the Calder became more powerful.

Ellie.

Present day, the year 2025.

"They're coming!" was all Ellie could say as she burst through the door, her eyes wide open in terror. Three bullets slammed into her back, the force of the impact throwing the tiny teenager across the room. Laro ignored the danger and ran to her, she was everything to him. Hyodo, although as horrified as the rest of the group, knew it was futile. The bullets hadn't penetrated all the way through her. They were fragmentation rounds that would have broken up in her body, lacerating every internal organ. If she wasn't dead now, she would be within seconds.

These were the bullets used by the Special Security Police, they were the 'safer', 'kinder' bullets, designed to fragment so that they wouldn't pass through a body and cause collateral injuries to potentially innocent bystanders. At least, that was the line fed to the public, though everyone knew their real purpose, they were designed so that even the poorest shooter would be a guaranteed kill shot.

No sooner had Ellie crashed to the floor, when an olive green cannister rolled in, Hyodo knew what this was too, it was an enhanced stun grenade. He had two seconds to prepare himself, and there was no time to warn his friends who were frozen in fear. He dropped down behind a desk, closed his eyes, put his fingers in his ears and breathed out. He kept his mouth open knowing the concussion from this iteration of flashbang could rupture his lungs if he held his breath.

There was a deafening bang and a blinding flash of brilliant white light. The pressure wave knocked him sideways tipping the desk over in front of him. But the munition hadn't finished, in a microsecond, a cluster of smaller flashbangs ejected by the first blast filled the room and detonated, sustaining the pressure wave. He heard the cries of his comrades as their eardrums ruptured; the pitiful squeals of the teenagers just a few years younger than him. But their pain wouldn't last long, the SSP squad burst in and started shooting. They couldn't see him, and he couldn't see what they were shooting at, but the screams told him all he needed to know.

Off to one side was an open doorway into another room, and in there was an open window; if he was lucky he could make his escape through it. The machine-gun shooting had stopped and moans from the injured were being silenced with single shots. These gun shots and tragic begging for mercy covered the sound he made as he dragged himself through the door. He stopped and listened, there was silence for a moment, save for the shuffling of military boots on the floor.

Squad leader Yadav spoke into his communicator, his distinctive, abrasive voice sending a chill through the already terrified Hyodo. "Squad A. Dhazi Noran not present, all others eliminated."

Hyodo hoped the squad had shouldered their weapons, but he heard footsteps approaching. The squad clearly had orders to kill everyone, so it was now or never. He had no choice; if he stayed they would find him and he would die. He ran for the window, diving through just as a squad member entered the room. The officer raised his weapon and fired; bullets raked up the wall and across the window. A bullet hit the heel of Hyodo's shoe, shattering, sending a shard through that cut across the sole of his foot. He didn't feel it, he wasn't even aware he had been hit as adrenaline surged through his veins, numbing him and giving him the strength to run.

The officer went to the window, raised his weapon and took aim. He was about to shoot when the commander pushed the weapon down, then looked at the boy through powerful binoculars.

"Leave him, he's not the one we want."

<<<<>>>>

Hyodo had gone a hundred metres, zigzagging down the labyrinth of side alleys before the adrenaline wore off and the pain exploded, sending him crashing to the ground. He dragged himself behind a garbage dumpster and examined his foot, only then did he feel the wet and saw the blood that had sprayed up onto his ankle. He cautiously looked back into the alley, there were splatters of blood everywhere - his blood, and he knew their dogs would easily be able to track him. But for the second time in ten minutes, he knew it was dangerous to remain here. He had to get to Dhazi and let him know what had happened. Ignoring the pain, he limped away.

An hour later and having satisfied himself that he hadn't been followed, he staggered into the meeting place where Dhazi was waiting. He limped towards the leader and collapsed in his arms.

"Where are the others."

"They're dead," cried Hyodo. "Ellie, Laro, Dano, Raja, and the others, they're all dead." Hyodo cried out in pain, Dhazi eased him into a chair noticing the blood around his shoe. He realised he had been shot with a frag round.

"I've got to get your shoe off. It's going to hurt."

"Do what you have to do," Hyodo gasped. Only then did the full horror of what had happened hit him. He burst into tears that quickly descended into a sob. "It should have been me, I should have died with them."

"You mustn't think like that." Dhazi was just holding it together himself as he stowed his feeling about the four friends that he would never see again and the others so willing to join his rebellion that he would now never meet. Ayeka entered the room, she'd heard everything. Though shocked, she went to Hyodo and put her arm around his shoulder to comfort him.

"It was the SSP," he gasped as Dhazi undid the laces of his shoe.

Ayeka knew she had to distract Hyodo as Dhazi tried to remove the shoe. "How did they find you?"

"I dunno, Ellie was on her way, they must have followed her."

"But Ellie was always so careful."

"She must have done something that alerted

them."

Dhazi tried to ease the shoe off, but Hyodo screamed.

"There's something digging in."

Dhazi looked at Ayeka. "Get him something to bite down on, this is going to hurt him."

She pulled off her thick leather belt and put it in Hyodo's mouth. Dhazi tugged at the shoe, Hyodo screamed again and Dhazi realised it was hurting him too much and he would have to cut the shoe off.

Ayeka realised what he needed to do and got a pair of scissors.

"Do what you have to," cried Hyodo. "It's what I deserve for surviving, I should have died in that room with them."

"Don't say that," said Ayeka as she stroked his arm.

"It's true, it's what I deserve. It was bad enough losing my parents, but now I've got no-one."

"You've got us, we'll look after you."

Dhazi cut around the uppers, separating them from the sole, then eased the two apart. He examined the cut, noticing that it wasn't as bad as they all feared.

"It looks a lot worse than it is."

Ayeka left then appeared a few moments later with a bowl of warm water, some clean cloths, bandages and a bottle of antiseptic.

"Leave it to me, I'll clean him up." A few minutes later the blood washed away exposing the small shard that had done the damage. "I've got to get it out. Bite down hard, this will hurt a lot."

Hyodo braced himself.

"Three, two, one."

He screamed again as she pulled out the bullet fragment, holding it up for him to see.

"Sorry Hyodo, it ain't over yet, the bullet went through the heel of your shoe and has probably picked up dirt. I've got to clean the cut or it will get infected." She turned to Dhazi.

"Get him up on his knees so the cut is up, then I can pour something directly in."

Dhazi positioned him, holding him tight.

"Are you ready? bite as hard as you can, coz' this is going to sting like a bitch."

"Just get on with it."

Hyodo tensed, gasped, but did not cry out.

With his wound cleaned and foot bandaged, the shock at what had happened to their friends hit them all hard. They had persuaded Hyodo to tell them exactly what had happened, hoping this would help him, but it seemed to make him worse.

Ayeka sat in silence. Ellie had been the youngest and Ayeka had persuaded the girl and her friends to join them. But the weight of the loss sat heaviest on

Dhazi's shoulders. It was his idea for them to meet there, but at the last moment his boss had told him that he had to work late, and he hadn't been able to contact any of the group. It had been sheer luck that Ayeka couldn't get there either, if she had been then he would have lost the love of his life and the force that was driving him on.

After an hour of silence, Hyodo spoke. "I meant what I said. I deserved to die with them. I hope I never let you two down."

Dhazi placed his hand on his shoulder. "You won't, Hyodo, you're my oldest friend, you me and Ayeka, we're tight, we'll support each other."

Hyodo looked at him, tears in his eyes. "But I might," muttered Hyodo as he took himself off to his room. Dhazi and Ayeka went to bed but neither wanted to sleep. Ayeka cuddled down and looked into his eyes.

"What do we do now?"

"You mean, what do we do about Calder?"

"Yeah."

"We carry on, we have to, otherwise their deaths will have been for nothing."

<<<<>>>>

Ayeka woke to find Dhazi by the window. The sun had just broken over the horizon and he was staring towards the upper east side, the dangerous upper east side.

He turned to her. "I've made a decision."

"What is it?"

"I'm going to see Lutcher."

"Risky!"

"I know."

"Do you want me to come with you?"

"No, it'll be better if I go on my own."

Extermination.

Fourteen years earlier.

The harassment has been on the increase recently, people were being stopped and questioned by the police for the flimsiest of reasons. It was something that everyone was just having to put up with now. But Erik Noran had nothing to hide and was not going to let it stop an innocent trip to the park with his seven year old son Dhazi. As they made their way, Dhazi pointed over the road to some soldiers getting out of a van and heading towards an abandoned warehouse. Two of them had cylinders on their backs that had hoses running to tubes they were holding. Other soldiers were adjusting valves on the cylinders.

"What are those men doing, Dad?"

The father frowned sightly, well aware of what these men were going to do and wondering how best he could explain it to his son. "That's an extermination squad, they're getting ready to do their job."

Dhazi sniffed the air and turned his nose up. "Poo, what's that smell?"

Erik had also noticed the unpleasant smell. "There's a rat infestation in there. That's the smell they make. Not nice, is it?"

Dhazi shook his head then looked up at his father.

"What does infestation mean?"

"It means there are a lot of rats in there, too many."

"What are the men going to do?"

"They're going to get rid of them."

"Why?"

"Rats are vermin and cause a lot of damage, they chew everything to see if it's food, even electrical cables and that can start fires. But they also carry diseases that can make people very sick."

"What does extermination mean?"

Erik sighed, he had tried to keep the realities of life from his son, but also wanted to answer his questions truthfully. Dhazi sort of understood what death meant but had never seen anything die. "It means that they are going to kill them all."

Dhazi's mouth curled down. "You told me that everything has a right to life."

"I know I did, but not everyone sees it that way. And sometimes these things have to be done otherwise they could get into people's homes and cause big problems."

"Can't they just capture them and release them somewhere else?"

"No, there are far too many and they'll just come back."

"How are they going to do it?"

Before Erik could answer, the door to the warehouse was kicked open and the soldier wielding the flame thrower stepped forward, dousing the interior with twenty litres of sticky, burning fuel. Erik turned Dhazi away so he wouldn't see, but he couldn't stop his son hearing the squeals of the burning rats. Some of the wretched creatures, still on fire, emerged out of holes in the walls only to get hit with clubs by soldiers waiting there for them.

As Erik led his son away, a horrified Dhazi looked up at him. "Why did they have to burn them, Dad?" Erik knew that poisons could be used, and that disinfectant would remove any disease carrying organisms left behind. But he also knew that they were expensive, and the local council wouldn't use them. Instead they brought in a flame thrower squad from the army that did the job just as well and that they didn't have to pay for. But he couldn't tell his son that, Dhazi was too young to understand, but he did know about germs.

"It's not nice, but the fire will kill any germs left behind. Come on, let's got home, it's not safe now."

The warehouse was supposed to be empty, but something inside exploded. It was not a big explosion, but it was strong enough to blow open a side door. A stream of panicking rats gushed out like a flow of dirty water, spilling out onto the ground and spreading across the wasteland to the side of the warehouse. A second flame thrower operator stepped forward, spraying them with fire. The screeching, burning animals scattered in all directions, chased by soldiers with shovels trying to hit them. Some of them got away and started secondary fires in the rubbish strewn around the site.

Erik picked up the pace. Dhazi couldn't keep up, so

Erik picked him up and carried him as he ran. Dhazi looked back at the men bashing the rats to death, with others thrashing away at the burning garbage, trying to put out the fires that were starting to spread and looking like they might get out of control.

"I think burning's a horrible way to die," whimpered Dhazi.

"Yes it is. It has to be the worst way."

They were clear of any danger and Erik put down his shocked son. "Try not to think about it."

"I don't think I'll ever forget that."

Erik was not surprised by his son's comment, even at his young age, he had a way of seeing things that other kids didn't. Though he suspected that Dhazi hadn't noticed the police watching them. They had got in their car and were following them. They were about fifteen metres behind, the driver matching its speed to their pace. He sighed, this had happened to him before and he carried on walking as he waited for the inevitable.

He heard the engine speed increase; the car passed them, stopping about ten metres in front. Erik knew what was going to happen next, it wasn't his first time he'd been stopped.

An officer got out, an odd expression on his face, a mixture of glowering and gloating. He stood still, his huge frame blocking the path, his hand already on his pistol, ready to draw it. The other officer got out and stood on the other side of the car, positioning himself to stop them if they tried to go around.

The man on the path held his hand up to stop them, Erik's shoulders dropped.

"Stop right there," commanded the officer.

Erik stopped, closed his eyes and sighed, then noticed that Dhazi was pulling forward. "We have to do what they say."

"That's right son, you *have* to do what we say," sneered the police officer. He went to Erik and placed his hand on his chest, pushing him back against a wall. Dhazi was too young to understand that the police always had the upper hand.

"Leave my Dad alone."

"Shut up kid," snarled the officer.

"We've done nothing wrong," Dhazi protested. The other officer chuckled, then turned to Erik. "You've got a gobby kid there, better keep him in check or his mouth will get him in trouble."

"He's seven," sighed Erik.

"What's his name?"

"Dhazi."

"Well it appears that you haven't done a very good job in bringing Dhazi up, have you? You need to teach him some respect..." he glared at the boy, "...before someone else does."

Erik shivered at the veiled threat. Dhazi seemed to understand and said no more.

The police officer with Erik stood back, a smug look of superiority on his face as he looked at Erik who was now bowing his head ever so slightly.

"Identification papers!" he demanded.

Erik reached into his pocket and took out his ID card. The man snatched it out of his hand and took his time examining it, then took out his data terminal.

"Records check on Erik Noran," he barked into the microphone. The device held the entire police database, allowing instant justice to be meted out. It took a microsecond to find Erik's records.

The screen displayed an image of Erik, along with some documents. The man took his time, pointedly looking back and forth between Erik and the image. He then read through the text and shrugged when he saw the words, 'No outstanding warrants.'

"It seems that you have no history of criminality... yet."

"We're a law abiding family, Officer."

"Until you're not!" he snapped.

"Wh-why did you stop us? You're s-supposed to say why," stammered Erik, anxiety finally getting the better of him.

The officer scowled and moved in close. "Oh, know the law do you? Do you think you know the law better than me, huh?"

"No Officer, I was told it the last time I was

stopped."

The officer sneered. "Well, since you know the law," he jeered. "We saw you looking at the army vehicles, you weren't taking down registration numbers were you?"

"We were just watching the fi…"

"Because recording the numberplates of military vehicles is a serious offence, a very serious officer," interrupted the officer. "Turn out your pockets."

Erik knew He had no choice but to comply and showed he had nothing. "My son was just curious."

"Curious, was he?" The man bent down and spoke directly to Dhazi. "That's dangerous, you should learn to be a little less curious in future. It could get you in trouble."

The officers got back in their car and drove away to find someone else to harass. Erik took hold of Dhazi's hand "Come on, let's just go home."

The young boy could see the effect that the confrontation had had on his father as they trudged along.

"Why were they nasty like that Dad? Aren't they supposed to be on our side?"

"Yes, they are supposed to be, but some of them like to abuse their power." *All of them like to abuse their power, Calder encourages it!* he thought to himself.

"What does 'abuse' mean, Dad?"

"It means having power but using it in the wrong way, a bad way."

"But why do they do it, Dad?" Dhazi paused and thought for a moment. "It's because they can, isn't it, Dad?"

Erik sighed. "Yes, it's because they can."

Dhazi's young brow furrowed. "One day somebody will change that."

"One day," muttered Erik under his breath.

Kari didn't need an explanation as to why they were home so soon, she could tell by the look on Erik's face. The Noran's were just another Matrean family trying to get on with their lives and raise their only son. Erik worked in a factory and Kari was a stay-at-home mother. There was no fear in the home, they were just resigned to living with the evermore restrictive laws that were being imposed.

"Harassment again?" she asked, knowing what the answer would be.

"Yes. I had hoped it would be a few more years before Dhazi saw it."

"Well, it's getting worse, so the sooner he sees it, the better."

"I don't see it that way."

"I do, he has to see what our world is turning into under this new Calder. It was bad enough under the previous one, when we were kids. But now..." she shook her head, sighing sadly. "I don't know what it's coming to with all these new laws. Soon it'll be illegal to be alive!"

Dhazi listened to everything that they said, taking it all in, storing it away.

The Teacher.

Three years later.

Miss Keiper stood at the head of the classroom looking affectionately at the eager faces of her ten-year-old students. Behind her on the wall, just like in every classroom in every school, in Matrea, there was a picture of Calder smiling benevolently. The teacher looked up at it with an expression of respectful admiration. She was from one of the rural areas and had worked hard for this job. Being a teacher in the city and so close to the palace had been her dream. Without Calder permitting it, her career would have been finished before it began.

Dahzi Noran sat next to his best friend Hyodo Simu. They'd hit it off on the first day of school and had been all but inseparable ever since, although neither of them were in competition with the other. Though they were in the same class, Dhazi seemed just that little bit brighter than Hyodo, and even at this young age had a leader quality about him. Hyodo didn't mind, he was more of the athletic type.

The teacher clapped her hands to get the class's attention. "Now children, get your workbooks out; I have a creative writing project for you. I want you to write a story about a person who wants to meet Calder, but they have to get from here to the palace without being seen. As you know, the palace is four kilometres away and there are many police officers on every street. You have a week to write it."

The children started scribbling away, all except

Dhazi, who sat staring into space. The teacher noticed.

"Can't you think of anything Dhazi?"

"I know exactly how I'll do it Miss, I just need to think through some details."

Two days later Dhazi handed in his story; four pages of what appeared to be a highly detailed plan. By the end of the week the rest of the stories were handed in. Miss Keiper took them home and sat with her husband reading through all of them, dismissing all except Dhazi's. She looked up at her husband. "You were right when you said we needed the mind of a child, this is perfect."

She looked up at her husband, both were members of the secret anti-Calder group, the 1027 Committee. It was labelled as a terrorist organisation. They saw themselves as freedom fighters, determined to end the dynasty that had ruled Matrea with an iron fist for a thousand years. Finding a way into the palace had been the long term aim that was finally coming to fruition.

A couple of weeks earlier they had captured one of the surveillance drones and reprogrammed it. As the drone was flying back, video images from it showed a weak spot in the defences. This was too good an opportunity to miss.

While all the other stories had people hiding in cars, Dhazi's story used the heavily polluted river. With no exceptions, all vehicles heading to the palace are thoroughly searched, so the river plan was the only one that had any chance of success. The story was memorised and then all were burned.

<<<<>>>>

On the following Friday night, at eight, and just as Dhazi had predicted, the northern industrial sector started to dump a weeks' worth of garbage into the foul-smelling, slow-moving river. In amongst the chemical and human waste there were many off-cuts of wood. A barrel would look like just another piece of rubbish.

The lithe female dressed in a black cat-suit, ignored the stench and the fumes as she lowered herself down into the barrel. Her husband handed her the pistol and a couple of magazines. She screwed on a silencer then looked up at him.

"This is either going to be freedom for all or goodbye forever. I love you."

The man held back his tears and forced himself to concentrate on the mission. He was the group leader and he had chosen his wife as she was the only one that could fit in the barrel. She had willingly accepted the mission. Her parents had been active 1027 Committee members and as a child she had witnessed their summary execution. Other group members had taken her in and looked after her, changing her name and getting false identification papers made. She had been driven by a sense of revenge ever since, but was playing the long game, using a teacher's role as a cover and constantly praising Calder to the children she taught.

Today would see the fulfilment of her dreams and Matrea would finally be free.

She hunkered down as he placed the lid loosely on top, knowing he may never see her again. He gave the barrel a little shove and despite of his hard-man attitude, he wiped away tears as he watched it float out of the side dock and into the main flow of the river that carried it slowly downstream.

The first checkpoint would be the easiest. Nobody wanted to be on watch on the bridge. Those duties were always assigned the new recruits, who would stay in their hut to avoid the smell and the vapours.

In the barrel, Keiper held a tissue to her nose, one that she had put a few drops of perfume on. That was only marginally effective against the stench and she had to work hard to control her vomit reflex. The chemical fumes made her eyes water, but her discomfort was worth it for the greater cause.

An hour later the smell had dissipated as tributaries had diluted the flow. A light clunking sound told her there was still plenty of detritus in the flow. Even so, she took a chance and slid the lid back a fraction, peeping up to see two officers patrolling back and forth, focussed more on the roadway than on the river. A boat would get their attention, no doubt about that, but floating debris, the kind that flowed past every Friday wouldn't interest them.

No-one had ever got this close to the palace before, and so far Dhazi's unwitting plan was working. As he had stated, the guards would watch the roads instead of the river. Keiper's heart pounded as she thought of getting into the palace and finally setting Matrea free. It would not be easy and she could lose her life, but she'd sworn an oath and this was her mission.

Soon she would approach a fork in the river where the natural flow would pull rubbish off to one side, leaving the cleaner water to head straight on to the palace. She took another chance and peeped out again, there were no bridges as far as she could see. Using the lid as a paddle, she silently guided the barrel away from the side until she was clear of the fork.

Her pace picked up, the river was shallower here and flowed faster as a result. Now, even in the darkness she could tell that fresh water was feeding into the river and water here was clear and without any of the foul odour. But the faster she went the more the barrel started to turn, slowly at first but getting quicker.

Using the lid, she slowed the rotation but could not stop it completely.

Dizziness set in.

The bottom of the barrel struck something causing it to spin faster, making her drop the lid which was carried away and out of her reach. She tried using her hands, but nothing she did slowed the increasing revolutions. She panicked, trying to recall the technique she learned at ballet class when she was a child, focussing on one spot for as long as possible, then quickly spinning her head to find the same spot. Though it was too dark now and she desperately searched all around, but the motion of the water made it impossible to find a suitable point.

The flow of the water had reached a speed where small whirlpools were forming up ahead, she was just able to make out one and tried to use her hands to steer away from it but failed. Trapped in the spinning water, she held on as the dizziness and disorientation built.

Eventually she passed out. She slumped forward the weight of her body upset the balance and moved the barrel to the edge of the vortex to be expelled from the spinning water. The barrel crashed onto the stony embankment, breaking up and throwing her out knocking her unconscious.

She woke to find the barrel of a gun aimed at her head.

<<<<>>>>

She was prepared for the beatings and stoically withstood three days of torture remaining silent between the blows, even when she was weak from lack of food and water. The beaters gave up and new interrogators entered the cell. She expected beatings but she was not prepared for the electric shocks, and within two hours had told them everything.

Twenty-four hours later every member of the group had either been shot dead or were in prison cells being tortured for information. She was executed first, with her husband forced to watch. She remained calm as the noose was placed around her neck, but just managed to shout 'Death to Calder' as the trapdoor opened. Then it was his turn to be hanged; defeated, he did not resist and made no speech. Eight other people were hanged that day. Homes were searched but the stories had been destroyed. The 1027 Committee was no more.

Although she had insisted that she alone had conceived the plan, Calder had his suspicions. This was too bizarre for an adult to have thought up; floating in a barrel was something only a child could have imagined. But even he couldn't make a move against children, though he made sure that tabs would be kept on every child that Keiper had taught.

Calder.

Calder looked out of the penthouse windows, slowly turning to get a panoramic view of Matrea's zones, the land his dynasty had ruled for forty generations. It had been four years since the failed assassination attempt, and the 1027 Committee had been crushed once and for all.

There had been no further attempts on his life, but there was always a possibility that one day someone could get all the way in. This was what the simulations had predicted, the simulations that he had ran hundreds of times every day since the doctors had told him that the gene was now active. Thousands of scenarios had all predicted the same outcome, regardless of the variables.

The palace was a huge pentagonal pyramid that dominated all of Matrea, and the penthouse was where he spent most of his time. This was where he made his plans, deciding which zone would be allowed to succeed and which zone would be held back. This was where he held court with those he permitted to be rich, those he allowed to think that they were rich and powerful. They were rich, they had money, but they had no power; any challenge to the accepted order would be dealt with by the praetorian guards.

When Calder's ancestors took control of Matrea over a thousand years ago, they formed the praetorian guard. These were fanatical loyalists that saw their duty as a calling and who swore absolute loyalty and devotion to the ruler. Fealty was too small a word to describe them. These were the only people he could completely trust, as he knew all would give their lives to protect him, such was their near religious fervour.

He viewed everyone else under him with suspicion, and rightly so. Traitors had always been a thorn in the side of whichever Calder ruled, and the praetorian guards had always been busy.

One kilometre from the palace, beyond the immaculately groomed gardens, the monuments and the statues of all the previous Calders, stood the perimeter wall a few metres high. There were no battlements atop for his men to hide behind during an attack. There were no machine gun towers to lay fire on an assaulting hoard. There was no need there had not been a mass attack on the palace for generations His oppressive rule meant that no-one would ever be strong enough to challenge him; strict laws harshly applied and brutal repression saw to that. The wall was just a symbol, a reminder of his power to all who gazed upon it.

He looked down at the statues; forty granite figures atop plinths, all depicting stern rulers. Beside each one was a monument listing all the laws introduced by that Calder. He had two monuments, one either side of his statue, one was complete, the other still under construction, with stone masons regularly adding to the list of increasingly harsh decrees he had issued. He often wondered if his successor would be as ruthless as him in maintaining order.

He thought back to his father, the previous Calder, who had let his grip slide and had tolerated resistance instead of crushing it. This had allowed The 1027 Committee to re-emerge, become powerful and grow to be a direct threat. But when his father died and he came to power forty years ago, he destroyed them. It took a decade for the bulk to be wiped out with only a few ineffectual groups left, but now even they were gone.

He had achieved domination by trebling the number of regular police, creating the riot police and the special security police. Draconian laws were passed with the promise that they would be repealed after 'order' had been restored, but they never were. Brutality by the security forces was common, it went unpunished and was even encouraged.

He fostered an air of selfishness and egotism amongst the population by discouraging social groups and successfully manipulating the media into portraying those who only looked after themselves as the new Matrean ideal. People who showed a civic spirit were branded as fools for helping the weak. Matrea was a spiteful place and would stay that way under his rule.

Beyond the wall were the zones. Despite never having been outside the wall, he knew most things that went on in the zones. Though not every last detail, the mundane minutiae of individuals' lives were of no interest to him. He just had a general overview that told him all he needed to know. It was four years since the teacher had been executed, and he had sensed a change back then, but he didn't know what it was. He just had a feeling that someone would grow stronger than they should. Though this was of no real consequence, the simulations had predicted that it would happen one day, and he had plans to deal with all foreseeable scenarios, this was just one of many, and he had a plan.

The West Zone had done particularly well over the past ten or so years, rapidly growing in wealth, and its relative prosperity was causing it to become a touch bourgeoise. He felt people there were filled with a sense of comfort – too much comfort for their own good, so maybe it was time for that zone to stagnate.

Prosperity had enabled firms to take on more staff than they really needed. Bloated levels of management had made the companies top-heavy and a touch too comfortable. It would be easy enough for Calder to engineer a change for the worse in the companies' fortunes, and a bit of redundancy amongst the middle class should take them down a peg or two. And as for the working classes, they knew their place, and a hefty chunk of unemployment would remind them of who the boss really was.

The East Zone was divided in two, the Lower East side and the Upper East side. The East Zone was always going to be rough, it always had been, there was no reason to change that. It was the oldest zone, housing there was poor and unemployment high. Calder allowed token developments there, with the suggestion that these would raise the living standards, but he also allowed vandalism to go unchecked. The east zone had the most crime; he kept the police numbers there low, allowing gangs to form and believe they were in control, thus keeping a depressive air to the place.

The vicious gang boss Lutcher held sway over the Upper East side, an area of five by five kilometres to the north of the east zone. The Upper East side was twenty-five square kilometres of extortion and violence. He controlled the pubs, clubs and music venues and the girls that worked the streets at night. Businesses paid him protection money and those that didn't ended up being burned down and/or their owners put in hospital. This was where the business owners and the well-off from the South Side came for their entertainment, whether it be music, gambling or girls. There were no theatres, no fine dining restaurants, just seedy bars, strip clubs, girls selling themselves on street corners and fast food joints that were all a cover for Lutcher's money laundering.

At twenty-five, Lutcher wasn't the youngest gang boss in Matrea, but he was the most violent, and Calder was well aware of all of Lutcher's activities.

Occasionally Calder would send in the feared SSP squads to do a sweep and instil a bit of terror. Streets would be sealed off and people dragged from their homes, homes that were then ransacked for no other reason than to terrorise the population. Fear was good, fear was the best weapon he had. Lutcher always kept a low profile during these visitations; he may have been charging protection money, but he couldn't protect anyone against the Special Security Police, he couldn't even protect himself from them.

Calder turned to look out over the river to the South Zone, which was mainly residential. This had always been the best zone, this was the place that had the art and culture, the museums, theatres and the zoo. This was the place where everyone wanted to live, if only he'd let them. The residents of the south zone were mostly the middle class, the merchants, the bankers, the lawyers, the small business owners. Housing in the western side of the south zone was more affordable and this was where the workers lived. It had its rough areas, but these were nothing compared to the North East zone. Division and rivalry were effective weapons that Calder used, and he did nothing to discourage the residents of all of the South Zone from having a feeling of superiority over the residents of the North Zone, and this blinded them to their own deprivations.

The south side had its own gangs, Orlo ran all of them. They were not as brutal as Lutcher's men, with Orlo preferring intimidation over violence, but when he chose violence, it was extreme. Providing each gang stayed on their side of the river, then there would be no conflict. There were invisible lines across the centres of bridges and tunnels.

It was not wise for the gang members on both sides to cross the demarcations. But there were frequent transgressions, with trespassers either accidentally or deliberately wandering into forbidden territory. Vicious fights ensued, and this suited Calder well. They were not situations that he had to plan, but something that he benefited from.

The Central Northern Zone was the industrial sector where the manufacturing industries were. The northwest zone was where the technology firms were located. The heavy industries drew its workers from the North East zone and the tech companies drew their workforce from the southwest; and provided there were no gang members, Lutcher permitted them to cross the river. That was what Calder allowed him to believe.

Calder's eyes fell on the central zone, the banking and administrative area with financial institutions and what passed for a government. He allowed the two-party system to give the illusion of democracy, but everyone knew he told both sides what to do.

One thing didn't exist in Matrea; drugs. Calder's ancestors had seen the damage that narcotics did to societies and made possession of even the smallest amount punishable by death, usually by summary execution. This law had been maintained into the modern era when medical opioids emerged. These were tolerated, but possession of these without a prescription or good reason was still a death sentence. Nobody risked it, not even Lutcher.

Balance. It was all about balance. Balance was the key, balance was the mantra. Balance was what had saved Matrea from oblivion ten centuries ago. Balance was what had to be maintained, no matter what the cost.

For every rich person there had to be a poor person. For every person doing well there had to be someone doing badly, and for every birth there had to be a death. Balance meant stability and maintaining stability was Calder's job.

Soto.

It was the morning of the race and Erik and Dhazi were getting ready. Kari, Dhazi's mother, would stay at home, she found the noise and smell of the motorbikes a bit too much.

An excited fourteen-year-old Dhazi grabbed the tickets. "Come on Dad, we're going to be late."

"We're hardly going to be late, there's two hours to go before the gates open."

"Yeah, Dad, but I heard that Soto is going to be signing autographs before the race, and I want to get one."

Erik Noran roughed up his son's hair. "You've already got his autograph," he teased, he knew that Soto was Dhazi's favourite rider; Soto was everyone's favourite rider.

"Yeah, but Dad, this is going to be his last ever race. He's retiring after this one."

The father chuckled. "So, which one of the *many* posters you have of him are you going to take for him to sign?"

"There's a new one, a special poster. I've been saving some of my credits for months now and I want to buy one of those for him to sign, can I, Dad? It's not too much."

"How many credits is it?"

"Twelve."

"Twelve! That is a bit much. You could buy a lot more with that."

"Please Dad, I really want it, it'll be special."

Kari threw her husband a knowing look. Her *'let him have it'* look.

Erik smiled, he was going to let him buy it anyway, but just needed to make his point.

"Okay, you can have it. But this has got to be the last one..." He laughed knowing what Dhazi was like. "...until the next time."

"Thanks Dad, can we go now?"

<<<<>>>>

Dhazi was buzzing with excitement as they walked to the circuit "Dad, did you know that Soto designs and makes his own motorbikes? He has his own factory and even makes some parts himself."

"Yes, I did know that." Erik chuckled as he remembered back to when he was Dhazi's age and he too was fixated on a sporting hero. Though in his day it was never so intense, and there wasn't all the merch to buy.

Dhazi swelled with a vicarious pride, keen to justify his adulation of the rider.

"Soto lets other teams use his designs so it's all about the rider's skill and not about the machine. He even gives some parts away, special parts that only the machines in his factory can make."

Erik had heard this from his son many times, but he didn't mind, there was so little for kids to do now, and he was happy that Dhazi had found something to occupy his mind. Though as they got close he felt his son's disappointment at the sight of the crowds waiting for an autograph. Dhazi ran to a merchandise stall, eagerly handing over the credits for one of the special posters and went to the side gate. Though as they drew nearer Erik soon realised that there weren't too many people waiting in the crowd and he let his son move to the front.

Dhazi's heart skipped a beat as a smiling Soto emerged through a door, the world champion looking sharp in his trademark white race leathers adorned with all of his sponsor's logos. Dhazi had pushed his way to the front and nervously held out the poster, Soto took it, unrolled it and took out a pen.

The boy's throat dried. "My name is…"

"Dhazi." Soto smiled as he signed the paper. "I remember you from last time, and the time before that. So, who do you think is going to win today?" Despite the fact that this race would be the pinnacle of his career, and he must have been feeling pressure, Soto's voice was kindly, like that of a favourite uncle.

"You're going to win, Soto," Dhazi whispered, excitement taking his voice.

"Possibly, but all the riders here today are talented, they wouldn't be here if they weren't. This is my last ever race and it would be good to win, though it is far from guaranteed. All my competitors are highly skilled, and they all want to win. They will not give way to me, and I would not want them to. If I felt that any of them had let me win, then my victory would be meaningless to me. No, I expect a tough race, and I want a tough race."

A wide-eyed Dhazi went to his father. "Soto remembered me! and he spoke to me! He said that even though it's his last race, he doesn't want anyone to let him win."

"That's called *'being magnanimous'.*"

"What does that mean?"

"It means he's being generous to his rivals. It shows great character and it is a quality to be admired."

"He's the best, isn't he Dad?"

"Yes he is, and in many ways other than racing. You could do well to follow his example."

"I will, Dad. I will."

<<<<>>>

The circuit was owned and maintained by the state, it was clean and modern with good facilities. Between the smells of machinery and oil was the smell of fresh paint, as there always was when they attended a race meeting. The state appointed management always said everything had to be freshly painted, as TV cameras would be covering every race.

Erik often wondered why The State was so keen for the circuit to be so well maintained when the money could be better spent cleaning up the East

Zone. Repainting every five races would be more than adequate. Deep down he knew it was just a distraction, a way of diverting the public's attention, making them feel that their lives were better than they actually were. Sport had always been used for this purpose, but Soto was different, he had charisma that was genuine. Erik kept his thoughts to himself as they made their way to their seats. This was a special day for Dhazi, one he'd been looking forward to for weeks, and had been talking about for even longer.

Dhazi and his father were positioned at the front, near the start and finish line, the ideal spot for a fan. "Soto's never lost a race at this circuit," said Dhazi as he fidgeted excitedly in his seat

Erik smiled at his son's hero worship. "He hasn't lost a race for the past two years, though there have been some close calls. It's the last race of the season so it's triple points for all the finishers and theoretically, there are a couple of riders who could still beat him. But if he wins today..."

"No Dad, it's not *if* he wins, it's *when* he wins!" interrupted Dhazi, indignant that his father could doubt the outcome.

"Okay, *when* he wins today he will make history.

The crowd roared as the riders made their way onto the track. Soto was last and got the greatest applause. He nodded respectfully to the crowd, then walked along the line of other racers, shaking their hands and giving them each a piece of the sash he wore when he won the world title the previous year. It was the traditional Matrean gift that symbolised good luck to the opponent.

As his chief engineer wheeled his bike out to the start line, Soto noticed Dhazi and went to him.

"I have seen you at many of my races, come to my factory tomorrow and I'll show you around."

The boy's mouth dropped open in shock.

Soto smirked. "I may even offer you a job when you're old enough." With that, the racer went to his bike and got ready for the competition which if he won would see him retire as the undefeated world champion and the greatest rider in history.

Dhazi stood stunned at his hero's offer, his father equally so.

Erik put his arm around his son and pulled him close. "Well you said you don't know what you are going to do when you leave school, but now you do."

The boy was overwhelmed and wiped tears of joy from his eyes.

"I wonder what he'll want me to do?" he whispered as emotion took his voice.

A hush came over the crowd as the lights came on signalling the riders to get ready. One by one they mounted their bikes, donned their helmets and had final words with their technicians. The engines started, the sound rising to a deafening roar that pulsed through the stadium thumping the crowd in the chest, before settling down to guttural throb. Soto reached over to shake the hand of his friend Matti, sitting astride his powerful Tachyon Racing motorbike. He was a rival from another team, but still his friend.

Matti was the only rider who could realistically challenge Soto for the title. Matti nodded to accept the gesture, they fist-bumped, then both riders dropped their visors and prepared to race.

As this was the last race of the season, in keeping with tradition, there would be a slow parade lap to start off with to let the riders acknowledge and thank their supporters. A green light flashed three times then went out, signalling the start of the parade. A wave of applause followed the riders around the circuit as they made their way back to the start line.

Soon the lap was completed, and all were in their grid positions, all lying flat to their machines ready to make the best start possible. The start and the first corner were crucial, and they all knew it.

Most riders had conventional bike designs like Matti's, with the fuel tank at the top that their chest could rest on. Some had Soto's design with the fuel tank below the engine and just a heatshield between the top of the engine and the rider's body. The higher centre of gravity made the bike lively and harder to handle but made it faster around bends. The conventional bikes were quicker in a straight line, but it was the corners that mattered, and Soto was the master of the corners, the only one who could properly handle the twitching machine through the twists and turns.

A ten-second countdown started with the tens

of thousands of race goers chanting, getting louder as zero approached. Bike engines were revved to deafening levels, the blue haze of exhaust fumes hanging over the riders. The engines screamed as the last three red lights went out and the green came on signalling the start of the race.

Matti dropped his clutch first, got the better start and at the end of the straight was in the lead by half a length, but Soto took him at the first bend. Behind them the rest of the field jostled for position with third and fourth place constantly changing. Soto was in the lead by five lengths as he rounded the corner into the fast finishing straight at the end of the first lap. Lying flat to his bike, he opened the throttle hitting his top speed in seconds as he thundered down the two-hundred metre long track. Glancing over his shoulder, he saw his friend Matti gaining on him. They were dead level with each other as they crossed the finish line to start the second lap. This was little more than a practice run for the final lap to decide the champion, and both riders knew it, both working out what they could do differently to gain that extra half a length.

Soon they were catching up with the tailenders, with Soto using his Bike's agility to weave through the field, and Matti using his Bike's sheer power to blast through. Time and time again the lead changed between them and with each passing lap Dhazi became more excited, yelling encouragement every time the two passed, even though he knew Soto couldn't possibly hear him.

Erik's pride forced him to hug his son, it was fantastic to see the boy so happy in the dreary world that they lived in. The boy had been depressed in the years since his teacher had been exposed as a terrorist. Erik had tried to hide the news of her execution, but the security police had visited the school and told everyone. That was four years ago, and Dhazi had struggled since then, but it seemed like Soto was helping him, particularly now as he has tomorrow's visit to look forward to.

With all riders pushing their bikes to the very limits, there were the inevitable failures and retirements, and as the thirtieth and final lap approached there were only twelve of the original twenty bikes still running. Ten were strung out around the circuit with Soto and Matti battling through the field, dodging past stragglers, oil spills and debris, neither rider more than five metres apart. The crowd were on their feet as Soto entered the final bend with Matti just three lengths behind. Ahead of them was the dead straight, two hundred metre sprint to the finishing line and glory for one of them. Both of them desperate to break the four-hundred kilometre an hour limit. Without the weight of fuel in their tanks, setting a new world record was a possibility. In less than thirty seconds they would know which one of them would be the world champion and new record holder.

A camera on rails beside the track, and a drone above, followed the two, relaying the drama to a huge video wall, the images switching back and forth between a side view and arial view as Matti inexorably gained on Soto.

"Come on Soto," yelled Dhazi as he saw the rider's speed displayed on the video. Soto was at 390, Matti was at 391. The speed of both riders was increasing, but Matti was gaining on Soto, the roar of the crowd drowning out the race commentators. Dhazi jumped up and down screaming with excitement. Looking back and forth at the video screen and the finish line it became obvious to him this was going to be close.

At fifty metres to go, Matti's front wheel was level with Soto's rear wheel, at thirty metres it was level with the engine, at twenty it was level with Soto's handlebars.

"Matti's going to win," gasped Dhazi, a sense of disappointment rippling through him. He stood transfixed, unable to take his eyes off the screen, which now showed the wheels in close-up. At fifteen metres to go they were level, and both had just passed the four-hundred kilometre an hour mark.

Suddenly, Soto's engine exploded. A piston burst upwards striking him in the chest, throwing him back and off the bike and onto the tarmac. Fragments of the cylinder head blasted out, hitting Matti sending him crashing into the side wall. There was a couple of seconds of stunned silence as the video feed showed both men's limp bodies sliding towards the finish, both stopping short as the blazing hulks of the bikes slid across the line. Video crews rushed forward, each one jostling for position, desperate to get the best close-up shot of the obviously dead Soto laying on his back in a pool of blood, his chest ripped open.

A feed from the drone camera was routed to the video wall, Dhazi's father spun him around so he wouldn't see the injuries. Mayhem erupted as the following bikes, whose riders were not fully cognisant of what had happened, ploughed into spectators that had rushed onto the track. Nobody was taking any notice of Matti who was writhing on the ground and obviously still alive. Dhazi managed to catch a glimpse of the people clamouring to get a look at the accident. Everybody wanted to see Soto's body, a morbid display of disrespect that even at his young age, Dhazi knew to be wrong.

Dhazi's father held him still as the crowd around them surged forward. They didn't want to see, so walked out against the tide of the ghoulish rabble. The path of his life had changed, only he didn't know by how much.

The boy cried for two days; it was his first experience of the death of a human being, it wouldn't be his last.

A Design Fault.

On the evening of the race, Soto's chief engineer, the team boss responsible for the engine build and the final safety checks, threw himself off the top of a twenty story building. There was no suicide note, but investigators who interviewed him in the immediate aftermath of the accident reported that he was distraught and inconsolable.

Four days after the accident, the investigation was complete and the report was made available to the public. Erik turned on the TV, coming in halfway through a special on the race accident.

'...*Soto was riding his own bike, one he had designed and was built in his own factory, I might add, and was clearly pushing it way beyond its limitations, and it is also clear that there was a major design flaw.*'

The broadcast was a talking-heads style of program after the main news, where experts would discuss in detail a current news story, and no news story was bigger than the death of Soto. The expert in question was Nakamo, the Founder and Chief designer for Tachyon Racing, the company that supplied Matti's bike.

'*Analysis has shown that in all certainty there was a fracture in the connecting rod between the crankshaft and the piston, and that it failed under the excessive stress during the final stretch. Looking at the recordings, as I have done many times, and from all angles, it is obvious that Matti was going to win. He had the faster bike and had been gaining on Soto all the way along the finishing straight. By the time he drew level, Soto must have realised that there was no way he could have won, and he should have backed off, thereby reducing the strain on his obviously flawed engine. That would have been the right thing to do, the honourable thing to do. If he had done so, then both riders would still be with us.'*

Nakamo sighed and shrugged in a way that was to Erik, clearly fake.

'It is obvious to me that the chief engineer knew of the faults and maybe that's why he committed suicide. He must have felt enormous guilt that his employers' poor designs had contributed to Matti's death, and that is truly lamentable. Especially since Matti was plainly going to win, and now we know that his bike was clearly superior.'

Nakamo had a faint hint of satisfaction over the removal of Tachyon Racings' main competitor. Though he was trying to hide this behind a look of sadness over Matti's death. Dhazi didn't notice the tone of voice but his father did. It was no secret that Tachyon Racing had tried to get Soto's designs banned. Erik could see the way the discussion was heading. This man was callous, but then again, Matrea was a callous place, a place where empathy was frowned upon while narcissism and self-serving attitudes were admired. He looked over at his son, wondering how he could protect the boy from this cold-hearted world.

'At Tachyon Racing, we use advanced computers that model all the stresses and strains that the engine will experience. By using such methods we can totally guarantee the integrity and reliability of our engines well beyond their maximum performance level. And that is why

we have never had a failure. Because unlike Soto, we don't rely on our gut, or the 'if it looks right it is right' attitude.'

'I would go so far as to say that Soto should be posthumously investigated for manslaughter of Matti through criminal negligence.'

There was a commercial break in the program that featured a lengthy advert for Mercury Motorcycles, the street legal versions of Tachyon race bikes that were soon going to be available to the general public.

Tachyon would have paid a lot of money to the TV company for the advert, and because of that, and despite this being a news program, the interviewer was obliged to avoid any controversy and to paint Tachyon in a good light.

'What do you think should happen to Soto's bikes that are being used by other teams?'

'Well, they are obviously dangerous and should be banned from use. I myself have ridden one, and even though I am a highly experienced and skilled racer with a great many wins under my belt, I found it very difficult to handle. Of course, now that we know that there is a serious fault with the design, the ban should be immediate.'

Nakamo paused for a moment, the interviewer didn't jump in with a question, and it seemed to Erik that this short gap had been rehearsed.

Nakamo frowned slightly, appearing to be thoughtful, but Erik could see the arrogant smirk behind the concerned expression.

'Soto always claimed that the bikes he supplied to

other teams were identical in every way to his, but having ridden one, I am now questioning that. The handling of the bike I rode was extremely poor, to the point of being dangerous, so I wonder if the steering geometry was different on his personal bike. We all saw how easily Soto was able to weave through traffic, and perhaps that is how he was able to win – by supplying inferior machines to his opponents, machines that we now know to have a lethal defect. There is a word for that, and I would say that word is 'cheating', wouldn't you? I can see no other way that Soto could have won so many titles other than he was a cheater and had been a cheater for all of his career. I must say, he hid it well, but now we know the truth, don't we?'

Though obliged to at least appear to be neutral, the interviewer made a barely perceivable nod of agreement.

'Thank you Nakamo for coming on and explaining all that to us.'

Nakamo nodded to accept the thanks, all the while hiding the triumphalism that he felt. In sowing doubt over Soto's character he ensured that even if Soto's designs weren't banned, the bikes would be abandoned by the teams. Tachyon were the only other manufacturer with the ability to produce race winning bikes in sufficient quantities and everyone would want them now. As the camera panned away from him, a slight smug smile broke on his face. Erik grunted in disgust.

The interview ended and the presenter turned to look directly into the camera. *'Given this information, it now seems that Soto was not the paragon of virtue that he always made himself out to be. Call in and let us know what you think. But stay tuned for an exciting documentary on the history of Tachyon Racing.'*

If the ban was implemented, it would enable Tachyon to dominate the races from now on. Nakamo had not been a good actor, and even though Dhazi might not have seen it, the man's gloating was obvious to his father. Erik turned the television off, sickened at the crass charade he had just witnessed, and was not happy that his son had seen it. Dhazi would certainly hear plenty of speculation about it at school, where everyone knew he was a fan.

Dhazi sat in silence for a few minutes, then got up, went to his room and ripped down all his posters of Soto, gathered up all the memorabilia and threw it in the garbage bin. Dhazi never again mentioned Soto or expressed any interest in motorcycle racing.

The Restaurant.

Six years later.

"You know the score, your job is to meet people when they come in. You greet them with a smile, ask if they've reserved a table, if they have, show them to it, if they haven't, check the seating and show them to a free table. You give them a menu each and take a drink order, blah, blah, blah. Everything is like you've done before, when they leave you clear the table and wipe down with a cloth and spray and get ready for the next customer and remember to smile and call everyone 'Sir and Madam'."

The restaurant manager pointed to a circular table in a corner. "Never sit anyone at that table, no matter how busy we get." He noticed the curious look on Dhazi's face. "That's the one the cops like to have. They can come in at any time, and if they can't have that table it'll cause problems for me, and I get enough grief from them already. Anyway, once they're seated, the first thing you do is take a drinks order. You do everything for them quickly and make sure whatever they order is given priority, everyone else can wait."

The manager shuffled away. "It's bad enough having to give them food for free," he muttered under his breath, but loud enough for Dhazi to hear. It was his first day at the restaurant and he was in at the deep end. He had lied about having Waiting experience to get the job to avoid being sent to work in the steel mill.

Since leaving school he had worked in the foundry and although he never got close to the molten iron, he couldn't escape the soot, dirt and grime. After three years he'd had enough and quit. There were too many stories of lung-cancer related deaths.

The employment bureau looked at his qualifications and work experience and had found him a suitable position – in another steel mill, the kind of work that he was desperate to get away from. He passed the restaurant on his way back home from the office, and on an off-chance had gone in and asked about vacancies. Whatever he'd said to the manager had worked.

That was yesterday, and now the twenty year old Dhazi would be starting his first day working the front of house in a mid-level food establishment. The pay was okay, less than he was used to, but worth it to not have to breathe in the acrid fumes and smoke again. Maybe the smell of steaks cooking would become a bit nauseating after a while, but at least they wouldn't be poisoning him.

One of the chefs approached him. It was Pauli, someone he remembered from school, a boy he used to be wary of, but who now seemed to have mellowed. He slapped a friendly greeting on Dhazi's back.

"I've been in the kitchen for three years now, yeah, it's hot and uncomfortable, not nice and cool with the air-con you have out here." He gave Dhazi a wry, knowing smile and pointed into the kitchen. "But I tell you this, I'd rather be in there than out here. Good luck."

A little ripple of apprehension flowed through

Dhazi, he wondered if Pauli was trying to warn him or was just having a laugh at the new guy's expense.

Service had been steady throughout the day, and despite having lied about his work experience, Dhazi had been to enough places like this to be able to bluff his way. Customers seemed happy with the way he treated them, and the manager, who had been watching him, was also pleased. There were three other front of house staff, and all worked well together.

Come eight o'clock the restaurant started to fill, by eight-thirty all tables were taken, except for the one in the corner.

Dhazi had to turn a couple of customers away, saying that they were fully booked and lied when they pointed to the empty table, saying it was reserved, and skilfully deflecting them when they pointed out the lack of a reserved sign.

All was going well, and Dhazi was confident that he could make a go of this, feeling that he had a natural way with people, something that his former job hadn't enabled him to explore. People were happy, chatting while they ate but all that changed at nine-thirty when six police officers came in and sat at the corner table. The relaxed air instantly changed, the chatter died down and a few people asked for their bill.

Dhazi went to the table and handed over six copies of the menu. "What drinks can I get you, gentlemen?" he asked in the most respectful way he could.

Despite obviously being on duty, the men all ordered beer. One of the men had a voice that he recognised, he was the policeman from all those years ago and on the day the rats were burned. Dhazi hoped the man would have forgotten him. He got the drinks and returned to the table, remembering which officers had ordered specific beers and placed them down in front of them.

"What's your name?" demanded the man from his past.

"Dhazi, Sir."

The man turned to his colleagues. "I once met a kid called Dhazi, a bit of a mouthy brat he was." The man turned back to Dhazi, sneering. "It weren't you, was it?"

"Probably not, Sir. Dhazi's a common name, Sir."

"That's good, 'cause we don't like mouthy kids, but I like you, so you're going to be our special waiter whenever we come in."

Ayeka.

Dhazi was walking home after his shift at the restaurant, grumbling to himself about the abuse he had received from Calder's riot police. The same abuse he had been getting for the past three months. They had set up at their usual table and were as loud and obnoxious as always.

He was not far from home when he heard a banging sound coming from a side alley. He glanced in and saw a girl he used to go to school with. He'd seen her at school every day but had never spoken to her. Even though he found her attractive, he'd never plucked up the courage to ask her out. The banging was her punching the side of a dumpster. He went to her, gently taking hold of her fist, stopping her.

"Whatever the problem is, it's not worth breaking your bones over."

She looked at him and her anger seemed to fade, she made one last punch with her other hand then turned to him.

"My Dad got beaten up."

"By the police?"

"Yeah, he's…" she saw the flashing blue light of a police car sweeping across the buildings opposite as it slowly approached the end of the alley. "Quick, kiss me!"

He wasn't quick enough, so she threw her arms around him, holding him tight and kissing him.

"Get a room!" shouted the police officer and laughed, hoping to have embarrassed them as he drove away.

She sighed as she let go, he's gone." Then she saw the confusion on Dhazi's face. "If we were just standing there talking, he'd have stopped and asked a load of questions, and I really couldn't face that, not today, and you've seen how hard I can punch. We'd have been in a lot of trouble."

"Do you want to talk about it?"

"No, not really, I'd only get mad again."

"What's up with your eye?"

"Ah, I had a scrap with a girl. I won. Hold on, I've just recognised you, you're Dhazi Noran from school."

"Yes, and I only know your first name, it's Ayeka, isn't it?"

"Yeah, Ayeka Beka. Why haven't we spoken before? I always thought you were quite cute." She looked him up and down. "And you're even better up close."

He coughed and blushed, and she laughed as he shuffled awkwardly. He cleared his throat that had suddenly gone tight. "I really liked you, and I really, really wanted to talk to you, but I didn't because I thought you were, you know, out of my league."

It was her turn to blush. There was a moment of silence, then she smiled coquettishly and with a twinkle in her eye. "Do you want to hang out with me?"

His heart skipped a beat, in all the times he's admired her from afar, he'd never imagined that she would say that to him. "Well, yeah. It's my day off tomorrow, you can come over if you want."

"Yeah, I'd like that."

"Dad will be at work and mum's going out shopping, she always makes that last all day. We'll have the house to ourselves, and we can do whatever we want."

She smirked in a way that he couldn't quite read. "I'm pretty sure we can think of something to do. But look, I've gotta go now." She smirked again. "Ah, I think I can hear another cop car coming."

She put her arms around him and kissed him again, only this time it was real and passionate. They stayed in an embrace for a while before she broke away and chuckled. "Oh, what do you know, there wasn't a cop car after all.

"Where do you live, Dhazi?"

"Apartment twenty-two, it's halfway along thirty-fourth street."

She laughed. "That's just two streets away from where I live, and we've never seen each other! Unbelievable. Come on, let's go" She put her arm around him as they made their way to the Lower East side, eventually getting to the corner of thirty-second street.

She turned to him, looking into his eyes for

a moment and with a curious expression on her face. She was smiling, but there was something else, something he couldn't quite read. "Back in school, if you'd have asked me out, I'd have said yes, and ever since then I've been hoping that we'd meet."

She gave him a quick goodbye kiss and walked away, looking back over her shoulder, giving him a little wave. He watched her until she disappeared from view, then shook his head, unable to believe what had just happened. The girl he had dreamed about for years had just kissed him and *she* had asked *him* to hang out with her. Suddenly the depressing air of Matrea didn't seem so bad, and if it wasn't for the ghastly job he had, he wouldn't have been walking along that road and might never have met her.

<<<<>>>

Ayeka laughed as she flopped back down on the bed. "Whoops, we just had sex."

Dhazi forced a frown. "And we don't have a permit. So the best thing we can do is to go to the police and hand ourselves in."

She laughed with exaggerated sarcasm. "Yeah, that's a great idea. I'll say you were asleep but had forgotten to put any clothes on. I'd snuck into your home so I could have a shower, but when I came out I caught the towel in the door, I slipped, fell on top of you, and we accidentally had sex."

"Totally believable! They'll go for that."

She stroked the metal tube under her wrist.

She'd had just over two years left of her mandatory contraceptive implant. Another level of control Calder had over younger people. That and the sex permit civilians were forced to complete for each partner, the whole idea that someone had control over that was degrading. "Two years before I'm free. What about you?" she asked.

"Two and a half. I've got about two years and five months of the old sperm blocker left. So no chance of me getting you pregnant anyway."

Ayeka stared up at the ceiling. "If I can't get pregnant, and you can't get me pregnant, why do we need to have a permit to have sex?"

"It's just another level of control that Calder has over us. I've seen the form that you have to fill out, you have to list details of the person you're going to have sex with, it's degrading."

"So it's not like a blanket permit to have sex…" she noticed the smirk on his face realised the pun she had made and sniggered.

He laughed. "It's not even a quilt permit."

She slapped him playfully on the arm. "You know what I mean."

"It's a one-off, and you actually have to get a new permit for every new partner. The idea is that you'd only get a permit once you are married so you'd only ever need one."

So it's just a way of reducing pre-marital sex."

"Yep."

She laughed. "But what about the girls in Lutcher's zone and all their clients? The permit office would be busy with all their applications."

"Well they're hardly upstanding law abiding citizens, now, are they?" He liked her even more now, she was realistic about the world in a way that he hadn't seen in girls before.

She was silent for a moment as she thought through the implications of not having a permit. "How is Calder going to know who has sex?"

"He doesn't have to know, he relies on fear, like everything else he does!"

"Fear of what?

"People are afraid of what might happen if they are caught, or someone snitches on them, so they abstain."

"What does happen if someone's caught?"

Dhazi sighed. "I think it's a fine and a criminal record, so next time there's any sort of incident, the police haul you in and interrogate you first, even if you were nowhere near at the time. It's just an extra form of harassment."

A sly grin broke on her face. "I bet there's people without permits having sex all over Matrea right now."

"I do hope so."

She cocked her ear to one side. "I reckon if we

listen really hard, we might be able to hear them."

Dhazi rolled over to face her. "You're beautiful."

"Ah, you ain't so rough yourself."

He lifted up her hand and looked at the grazes on her knuckles.

"You could have broken your fingers punching that dumpster."

"Yeah, well, I was mad, and that was yesterday."

"Is your Dad going to be okay?"

"Yeah, it ain't the first time he's been roughed up and it won't be the last. When he was our age he made some public statements against Calder, so his card has been marked ever since." She huffed with an air of resignation. "Statements! That's all we can do, make statements and then accept the consequences, that really is all we can do, isn't it?"

"Not necessarily."

She turned to him, frowning but curious. "What do you mean?"

"How about we put some clothes on and talk about it."

<<<<>>>>

They sat at the table both sneering their noses up at the awful coffee. He shrugged.

"Sorry, this is the only coffee we can get."

"Don't worry about it, it's the same as we have."

She took a mouthful then put the mug down and pushed it away, grimacing. "Now, when I said that we can only make statements, you seemed to imply that we could do more, what do you have in mind?"

The longer he was with her, the more he was attracted to her. It went beyond liking, there were a lot of girls that he liked. He'd had a few girlfriends before, but she was different, she had a directness, a force of personality that set her above the others. If her father was a rebel, then maybe she'd inherited some rebel genes. She was a 'take charge' sort of girl, as she had proved earlier on when she pushed him onto the bed.

She looked at him and could see the man he could become. She saw the strength he had, the strength he didn't realise that he had. She'd had boyfriends before, but none had what Dhazi possessed.

They'd been with each other for less than twenty four hours, but he felt a strange feeling inside, it was new, and it was strong. He guessed what it was but had to resist voicing it. He tried hard not to make it too obvious, as there were more important things to discuss. Though she had a look about her. Their eyes met and there was silence for a few moments.

She smiled a knowing smile, a smile that showed her recognition of his feelings. "Yeah, me too," was all she needed to say. They stayed looking unblinking into each other's eyes for a few more moments. She took hold of his hand, they were in love and they both knew it.

"Right, we both know how we feel about each

other, so now we've got that out of the way, what is it you wanted to say before our emotions caught up with us?"

And there she was, forthright, cutting through to the nub of the matter without getting all dreamy. She was the one, something radiated from her, it was more than confidence and it was seeping into him. She was the one he wanted to be with forever.

She was aware of all that and smirked. "I believe in GSD."

"What's that?"

"Getting shit done."

He sat back and stared at the floor for a few moments, trying to come up with the right words. He had to avoid looking at her, otherwise his emotions would boil up and he might say something stupid, and this was too important. "How many kids do you know about our age that are fed up with everything, the rubbish jobs, the lack of prospects, the gangs, the police harassment?"

She shrugged. "Oh, I dunno, only about every single one I meet."

"Exactly! So what are we going to do about it?"

"Well, you tell me, because you've clearly got a plan."

"Yeah, I have. We talk to kids, we tell them to reject Calder's rules. We do small acts of defiance to start off with, though nothing that will bring too much hassle, but enough to get noticed. Though we don't go out on the streets, that'll be too risky, so we'll have to do it in the shadows. We build a movement and once we have enough kids on our side, then the adults will join in. It could get dangerous, but will you join me?"

"I will, because..." She leant over and whispered in his ear. "...I think we're going to be good together."

"Does that mean we're officially a couple?"

She grinned. "We had sex didn't we?"

He chuckled. "Well, we'd better go and get a permit then."

"Nah, let's carry on breaking the law. I mean, we're going to be breaking the law in other ways, so we might as well enjoy some of it."

Dhazi went to a drawer took out a small rectangular box and handed it to her. "I want you to have this."

She looked at him curiously, then opened it. Inside was a necklace, a fine silver chain with a small silver heart. He took it out and placed it around her neck. "It was given to me by my gran, she said I was to only give it to the girl that I truly loved and no other. I always hoped it would be you."

Ayeka lifted the heart and looked at it, speechless for a moment, then looked at him.

"Does this mean we're engaged?"

He shrugged. "Probably."

"I suppose I'd better tell my Mum and Dad then." She paused and thought for a bit. "Nah, not yet. Mum will want to start organising things. No, let's give it a while, we've got more important things to do." She nodded towards the bed. "But before we embark on our plan to bring down Calder, how about we break the law one more time?"

<<<<>>>>

They hadn't heard his mother come home from shopping early and didn't hear her coming up the stairs.

"Dhazi, I've got you some…"

Ayeka jumped off him and pulled the sheet up over herself as Kari opened the door.

"Ah, mum, you're home awfully early, we were just…"

"I know full well what you were just doing."

Ayeka peeped out from under the sheet and gave Kari a little wave. "Good afternoon Mrs Noran, erm, nice house you've got here."

Kari put her hands on her hips and frowned at her son. "Do either of you have a permit for what you've obviously been doing?" she demanded.

"No mum," he replied sheepishly.

"No, Mrs Noran," Ayeka replied, nervously biting her lip and getting ready to be shouted at.

There was an awkward silence for a few moments,

then Kari smiled. "Good, it's stupid law, so carry on. I'll be downstairs I'll put the radio on, because I don't want to hear anything."

A few minutes later a fully dressed Dhazi and Ayeka came downstairs, both cringing.

"Err, mum, this is Ayeka Beka, she's a friend."

Kari chuckled, amused at their embarrassment. "Well, I'd rather hope she is."

Unsure of what to do, Ayeka held her hand out awkwardly. "Pleased to meet you Mrs Noran." She blushed as her stomach rumbled before his mother could reply.

"Have you two had anything to eat?"

"No."

"Well sit down and I'll fix you something, no doubt your 'activity' has made you hungry."

Kari had noticed the necklace straight away, but they were halfway through the meal before she mentioned it.

"Ayeka, I see you're wearing the necklace given to Dhazi by his grandmother. It has a very special meaning."

"I know it has Mrs Noran."

"Good, so now that you are aware of its significance, you must call me Kari."

<<<<>>>>

"This is Ayeka, we're together," said a proud Dhazi as he introduced her to Hyodo. "We've been mates since school, haven't we Hyodo?"

Hyodo's eyes lit up at the sight of the confident young woman with her arm around his friend. Although Hyodo was the same age as Dhazi, she thought he seemed a bit younger, he appeared to have less confidence.

"Oh. Erm, wow," he stuttered, unsure of what to say.

"How did you? I mean, Dhazi hadn't mentioned you before."

She held her hand out, showing the marks on her knuckles. "We met last night, I was in a bit of a mood and was punching a dumpster. Dhazi stopped me."

Hyodo turned to Dhazi. "Well, remind me never to get on the wrong side of her." Then his eyes fell on the necklace she was wearing. He too knew the significance of it. She noticed the look on his face and knew to leave the two men alone for a bit. "Do you want a coffee, Hyodo?"

"Err, yeah, thanks." He took out a five credit note and handed it to her. "White with one, please."

"I'll get it." She handed the money back, got up and went to the counter of the coffee shop.

As soon as she left, Hyodo leant forward, lowering his voice. "I remember her from school, everyone wanted to get with her, and now she's with you, and you've given her the necklace. This is serious, isn't it."

Dhazi's shoulders dropped, and he sighed in a way that people only do when they're in love. "Yes, it is."

"Look, if you don't want me around, just say. I'll understand."

"Don't be daft, Hyodo, you're my oldest friend. Sure, I'm going to be spending a lot of time with her, but we've got plans."

"What sort of plans?"

Dhazi looked around nervously. "The reason she was punching the dumpster is that her father got roughed up by the police, and not for the first time, and let's face it, everyone's had enough of the harassment by Calder's police. We've got to do something about it."

"Like what?"

He lowered his voice "We're going to start a movement against Calder."

Hyodo's eyes lit up. "Like the old 1027 Committee? My Dad told me about them, but he said they'd gone away, and we mustn't ever talk about them."

"No, we'll not be out in the open like they were, at least not to start off with. We'll have to stay anonymous until we've got enough people on our side. Are you interested?"

"Yeah."

"Great, because we need you."

Ayeka returned. She handed over the coffee, then

looked Hyodo straight in the eye. "I guess Dhazi's told you about our idea."

"Yeah."

"What do you think?"

Hyodo scowled slightly, a look Dhazi hadn't really seen in him before. "Something's got to be done, there aren't many people who haven't been harassed, and it's getting worse. The cops leave mum and Dad alone..." he shrugged, embarrassed, then his shoulders dropped, and he looked sad. "...because, you know, there's no point with them."

Dhazi turned to the slightly confused Ayeka. "Hyodo's mum and Dad are ill, he looks after them."

She reached over and took hold of Hyodo's hand. "If you need anything, just ask, we'll help you."

He swallowed hard, touched by her gesture. "Thanks," he whispered, then sat up straight and smiled. "We don't need to be talking about your ideas here."

"Correct, we can only talk about them back at my house when mum and Dad are out. I don't want to involve them just yet."

Dhazi, Ayeka and Hyodo sat around a table. Erik was at work and Kari was out shopping, She had said that she would be out all day and that this time she would call before coming home. Despite his parent's lack of disapproval, the idea that Dhazi's mum had given them her tacit approval to have sex had turned them both off. Hyodo had been due to come over anyway.

Ayeka placed an old notebook on the table. "My Dad gave me this. He said that I had to be careful of who I showed it to."

Dhazi picked it up and flicked through the yellowing pages and caught the earthy, musky aroma given off by the breaking down of the cellulose and lignin in the paper. It was a strangely comforting aroma, it smelled like old knowledge. He noted that some pages had been torn out.

"What is this?"

"It has information on tactics used by the 1027 Committee, it's a playbook."

Dhazi immediately dropped it. "Wow, this is dangerous, just having it could see a person being chucked in prison."

Hyodo, intrigued, picked it up. "Why are some pages missing?"

"Apparently, they had the alias's and addresses of 1027 members. Dad tore them out and burned them."

"Yeah, but they can still read them from the indentations on the pages below."

"Yes, they can, which is why a sheet of metal was always placed between the pages when an entry was made."

"Your Dad was a member, wasn't he?" said Dhazi, knowingly.

"Yep, but he got out before it became too dangerous. But that's why he's always getting hassle. I've lost count of the amount of times we were dragged out of the house at four in the morning while the place was turned over. It's eased in the past ten years or so, but you know, every now and then the police are told to make a point. He never admitted to being a member, and no-one ratted him out, but back then suspicion was enough. And like I said before, his card's been marked ever since."

Dhazi took it from Hyodo and flicked through it again. Ayeka reached over and turned the page for him. "You need to read page five."

The page heading was 'Disruption', and it went on to detail the types of acts that could be used to interfere with police operations.

'Serious action needs to be targeted at police communications; once these are broken, no serious action should be taken for a while. Acts like these need to have a long gap between them and this will unnerve Calder, as he won't know what or when something will happen next. There will be harassing raids on the population afterwards, but that is a small price to pay.'

Dhazi half-smiled as he saw one method that dated the book; an instruction to stage an accident with a telegraph pole to break telephone lines.

Ayeka smiled, she had found that one quaint as well.

Dhazi thought for a bit. "We could still use this.

The communications are all done by satellite with multiple redundant systems, and we can't hit them all, but they all need power. We need to find a way of cutting off electricity supply."

He scanned through a few more pages, lingering on one that was a rough plan of how to attack the palace. He held up the book. "This is dangerous, we read it, memorise it then burn it. Agreed?"

"Agreed," they replied in unison.

<<<<>>>>

Dhazi and Ayeka quickly became inseparable, her spurring him on, lifting his spirits and making him believe in himself. When they discussed the 1027 tactics, an intensity would come over her, an energy seemed to emerge from her and flow into him.

"You can do it, you can lead us," she would say. "I see it in you, you can unite everybody and together we can bring Calder down."

Hyodo noticed the change in his friend, the confident look on Dhazi's face when Ayeka was standing shoulder to shoulder with him. The aura around them radiated out a power that he couldn't define. It was just that, a power, and it was good to see.

<<<<>>>>

They'd been together for about a month, Kari liked her, Ayeka was a practical, level-headed girl, and since they'd been together Dhazi had developed a focus. He seemed to have grown in stature, he had found the missing piece of his life. She was staying over a lot more now, and sleeping with Dhazi, something that his parents didn't raise any concerns about. They were realistic about life, and liberal in their thinking.

Ayeka dried the plates as Kari handed them to her. Kari glanced over at her son, then glanced at the young woman with a kindly look in her eye. "This is the furthest you two have been apart all day. I think it's time you got a place together, then you can start to live your lives without Erik and I getting in the way."

"But who's going to help you do the washing up, Mum?" laughed Dhazi.

Chores done, Dhazi and Ayeka went to his room. "Your mum's right, we should see about getting a place of our own."

"Yeah, I've been thinking that. I think we can afford it, though it won't be as nice as here."

"That doesn't matter, babe, it'll be our place." She became serious. "Our comfort isn't important, though, is it? It can wait, we have work to do."

"True, we'll get a nicer place when Matrea's a nicer place."

She rested her head on his shoulder. "It won't matter to me where we are, so long as I'm with you."

Just over a week later they had collected the keys to a flat and had just stepped through the door. It had two bedrooms, a bathroom, a kitchen and a living room with a door that led directly onto the street. All the rooms were small, and the area was close to the Upper East side, and as a result, the rent more affordable. It took over half of Dhazi's take home pay, but it was their own place.

Ayeka opened all the windows to let fresh air fill the space that had gone a bit smelly from being unoccupied for too long. Dhazi had used the unoccupied status as a means to haggle down the rent, and the landlord agreed, pleased to finally have an income from this property again.

Dhazi opened an envelope that his father had given him. Inside was a stack of credits.

Ayeka pointed at it. "How much is there?"

"Looks like around two hundred."

"Right. The first thing we're going to do is buy a bed. The two single mattresses that your mum and Dad gave us will be okay on the floor for a few nights, but a bed makes a home." She stopped and thought about her words and a slight dreamy air came over her. She smiled awkwardly, held him tight and rested her head on his chest.

"Dhazi, this is our home," she whispered, her voice uncharacteristically wavering with emotion.

Eventually she let go, went into the kitchen and opened the oven door, immediately recoiling from the smell of congealed fat and mouldy food from a saucepan that had been left behind. She shut the door and wafted the rancid odours away.

"No, actually, the first thing we're going to do is clean this kitchen, it stinks."

Dhazi had never done much in the way of housework before. His mother always wanted to do it, she said it was something she enjoyed, and while he watched Ayeka organising what few possessions they had, he understood why, though a thought came to him.

'How can she make cleaning look sexy?'

She smiled to herself, she knew what he was thinking.

<<<<>>>>

Hyodo became a frequent visitor; apart from Erik and Kari, he was the only other visitor. He was happy for Dhazi and never jealous of him, despite the love that his friend had found and his own circumstances that precluded any sort of romantic relations with a girl. Ayeka quickly found out the food that he liked and would often cook for him. He helped out by buying food when he could, but Dhazi knew he was struggling financially. His parents were too ill to work, and he was having to help them out with money. He was embarrassed by that and asked Dhazi not to say anything to Ayeka, but she knew.

In amongst the serious discussions, there were plenty of light-hearted moments, though Ayeka sensed a sadness underneath the relaxed attitude that Hyodo displayed. She chose not to mother him, it would have been easy, but wrong.

Eventually, Dhazi gave Hyodo a key, something that made him get emotional, and that was something

Hyodo had never done before.

Petrol Bomb.

Ayeka pulled out an old piece of paper with what looked like a recipe written on it.

Dhazi took the note. "What is this?"

"It's a recipe for petrol bombs."

Hyodo laughed. "Recipe? What do you need a recipe for? isn't the name a clue? You know, a *petrol bomb.*"

She frowned slightly and became serious. "If you just use petrol, it catches fire but just runs off, so unless it can soak in, or there's something that's going to catch fire quickly, it's no good. Too much risk for not enough damage." She pointed to the various ingredients. "These will all dissolve and make it stick to whatever it lands on, and it's difficult to put out. It will even stick to damp surfaces, providing they're not too wet.

Dhazi looked at her curiously. "Where did you get this?"

"My Dad. He's had it since way back. He said he never used it in anger but hung on to the recipe just in case. I think he always knew I'd grow up to fight against Calder." She thought for a bit. "We all agreed on disruption to start off with, so I think we should hit infrastructure first."

Hyodo frowned, suddenly realising just how serious she was being. "Like what?"

"Dhazi said we should target the power grid. We should go for a main distribution hub that feeds one of the zones." She tapped the recipe. "Hit it in the right place with a few of these and all the lights go out."

Dhazi shook his head. "No, that will hurt the very people that we need on our side, their lives are rubbish enough as it is, so we mustn't inconvenience them. The security forces have their own sub stations within the hub."

Ayeka shrugged. "So we hit those instead."

Hyodo looked doubtful. "I learned about generators in electrical tech' as school. They'll have backup generators at the station."

"Well, we hit those as well." She put her hands on her hips, cocking her head to one side. "Come on guys, you're being a bit negative."

Dhazi thought for a bit, then smiled at her. "Yeah, you're right."

"I usually am," she muttered under her breath, but loud enough for him to hear, then smirked as she looked at him, a twinkle in her eye.

Dhazi tried hard to focus, but it was always difficult when she looked at him like that. Even though Hyodo was present, his mouth still went dry. And he knew that she knew the effect she had on him.

Hyodo sniggered. "Shall I give you two a few moments alone?"

Dhazi blushed, shaking his head to get serious. "Okay, we'll hit the combined police and security services building. Hyodo, you know about electrical stuff, so you check out the location of the hub and see if you can work out what transformer sends power to the security building. The generators will be in the grounds of the building, so we need to find a way of getting inside the compound to find out exactly where it is."

Ayeka cowered down a fraction, bowing her head while looking up at him. "Please Mister," she whined using a feeble voice. "Me 'andbag's been stolen." She reverted to her natural voice. "Yeah, I can play the dim girl to get inside."

Dhazi shook his head dismissively. "No, they'll tell you to clear off, they won't be interested in the theft of a handbag."

"Oh, I can get them interested." She hunched down again, leaning slightly forward letting her top gape open. "I do this, and I guarantee they'll take me inside wanting me to make a statement."

Hyodo looked away, embarrassed. Dhazi didn't know whether to be shocked or impressed.

She looked at him and grinned. "I've got the tools, so I might as well use them."

<<<<>>>>

They went to the lock-up garage and experimented with small quantities of the recipe, adjusting the ratios until they felt it was just the right consistency. Dhazi studied the opaque liquid. "We need to test this. People are always burning rubbish on the waste ground to the rear of the garage, one more fire won't arouse suspicion.

They put a small amount into a bottle, put a rag in the top then went outside. There, a few metres away, was a large block of cast concrete. Dhazi handed the bottle to her. "It's your recipe, you do it."

She took it and turned to the both of them. "Dad always said you have to hold it the right way when you throw it. If you hold it with the open end behind you, when you chuck it the fuel shoots back and could dump out all over you. Not ideal, very not ideal. He said he saw it happen at a demo, a guy got covered in it and, erm, he didn't survive. What you have to do is hold it upright all the time and throw it, not over your head, but with a sort of sideways action, like this." She held the bottle and demonstrated the way to throw it, the way her father had shown her.

Hyodo lit the rag. She threw the bomb at the block. The bottle broke at an angle, spreading a smear of the raw fuel mixture along the concrete until the rag ignited it. The flame raced back and in an instant the whole metre long strip was alight, burning with bright yellow flame and giving off thick black smoke.

The gel formed by the ingredients held the flame, and after about thirty seconds the mixture started to melt and slide down, creating a sheet of fire. Two minutes later all the fuel had burned away.

Hyodo bounced around excitedly. "Did you feel the heat that stuff gave off?"

Dhazi was impressed, he looked at her curiously. "You've done this before haven't you?"

She grinned. "Yeah, I've practiced. Dad said it would be an important skill for me to have. He said I might need it one day, and what do you know? I do."

"Okay, now we know it works, we just have to scale it up, then check out our target."

<<<<>>>>

Hyodo strolled casually along the track to the side of the combined police and security headquarters. He was a fair distance away, so would only draw casual attention, if he drew any attention at all. He had his head down and was pretending to read a book, but his focus was on tracing the power lines.

He tracked them out of the building until they joined the multiple cables on the power distribution pylons. This could have been an issue, but he had noticed that the ones to the security building had a ring of yellow paint every five or so metres.

Following the pylons was now impossible, as they disappeared out over fields. He reasoned that the yellow rings were to indicate to electricians that this supply was for the police building and because of that he further reasoned that it would tell him which part of the substation was dedicated to it. He knew where the power came into the East Zone, it was into a huge substation on the eastern edge. He went to his home, got his bike and his father's old binoculars and went for a long ride.

The power distribution hub was massive, but through the binoculars he saw the cables with the yellow paint splitting off to a smaller transformer. It was a grey cube much smaller than the rest of the ones feeding power into the East Zone. It was about the size of a garden shed but made of metal with numerous tubes at the side emerging from the bottom and entering again at the top. He remembered his technology lessons and knew that these contained oil as a coolant. This was where they had to strike.

Keen not to spend too much time obviously studying the hub, he got back on his bike and cycled back to Dhazi's flat.

<<<<>>>>

Dhazi walked with Ayeka until they were nearly at the building. As planned, she wore a revealing top and skin-tight leggings. They made her look as if she had been dipped in grey paint. Nothing was left to the imagination. "Are you sure you want to do this?"

She gestured in the direction of the building. "I've got a pretty good idea of what the guys in there will be like. "Dhazi chuckled. "Unless you get a cop who's secretly gay and he's not interested."

"Nah, there's no gay cops, it's illegal, remember? So no-one's going to take that risk, and even if one of them is gay, they'll pretend to be interested."

"Okay. I'll wait here, but please be careful."

She gave him a kiss then adopted the demeanour of a vain, self-absorbed girl only interested in fashion, the type that she now saw too many of in Matrea. She left him and made her way to the building.

<<<<>>>>

"I wanna report a feft."

The desk sergeant sighed. "You mean a theft."

"Yeah, that's what I said, didn't you 'ear me?"

"Okay, what was stolen?"

"Me 'andbag."

"Were there any valuables in your handbag?"

"Like, make-up, new phone, I'd only had it for, like, a couple of days, then there's me 'ouse keys, an' like, a few creds."

"Have you got any ID?"

"Nah, that was in there an' all, weren't it."

"When was it stolen?"

"Like, yesterday?"

"Okay what's your name?"

"Li-ann Matsu."

The sergeant pointed to a chair. "Okay Li-ann, wait there and someone will see you shortly."

After about forty-five minutes a young detective, one that she assumed to be fresh out of training college, approached her. She looked at him, he was perfect. He was obviously new and would be given the most trivial crimes to investigate. It was exactly what she had hoped for. As he got close, she pushed her chest forward, making her top pull tight across her chest, but made it look like her natural pose and pretended not to notice his eyes fall on her cleavage.

"I am Detective Drumetski, come with me, please Miss."

She followed him, all the time glancing into rooms trying to spot where the backup generator might be. He took her to an interview room, she sat opposite the man. She avoided eye contact, looking everywhere but at him so that he could look at her chest and think she didn't know he was doing it.

He read through the notes the desk sergeant had made. "Where do you think your handbag was stolen?"

"It was like, on the bus, weren't it. One minute it was there, the next it was, like, gone."

"If you had valuables in it, why weren't you holding on to it?"

"I was like, waving to my mates outside, weren't I."

The detective sighed. "Can you give me a description of your handbag?"

He opened a file and made a note of the description, missing out all the times she said 'like' then looked at her. He was bored with looking at her chest and wanted her out of the way so he could get on with a crime he might even be able to solve.

"I think you can appreciate that this is low priority for us. You will have to go to the council to get a new ID card." He looked at the notes again. "You stated that your phone was new, was it expensive?"

"Yeah, it was like, four 'undred creds."

"Had someone on the bus seen you using it?"

"Well, yeah."

"That was why your bag was stolen - to get the phone. It would have been sold on by now." He filled out a form and handed it to her. "This is a crime number so you should be able to get your phone replaced on insurance."

Her face dropped. "Oh, the paperwork for that was like, in me 'andbag an' all."

He sighed again. "Speak to the shop you bought it from, they might have a copy of the insurance document."

"What about me make-up, I ain't got none." She pointed to her un-made up face. "I can't go out like this."

"You'll have to buy some more."

"But I ain't got no creds now."

"We can't help you with that." He stood up and gestured to the door. "Come back in a week or so's time and I'll let you know if I've found anything."

She went to the door and deliberately turned the wrong way, walking swiftly away from the entrance, glancing in rooms as if she was lost.

"Wrong way," he shouted after her.

"Sorry," she muttered as she skuttled past him.

"Stupid bimbo," he grumbled as he watched her

leave the building. He would place her file at the bottom of his DNB stack, the 'do not bother' pile.

<<<<>>>

"Well?" he asked anxiously. "You were in there for quite a while, I was starting to get worried.

"It was easy, and I knew I'd have to wait."

He gestured awkwardly at her chest. "Did it, you know, work?"

"Oh hell yeah, as soon as he saw me he took me into an interview room. He couldn't keep his eyes off me."

A little wave of jealousy hit him. "I'm not sure how I feel about that," he muttered. She recognised it and stroked his arm.

"Don't worry about it babe, it's just that we've got to use every resource that we have."

He coughed to cover his embarrassment at feeling jealous when she had put the project ahead of any qualms she might have had about using her body.

She grinned at him. "Once I was into the main part of the building, I saw one of those emergency site evacuation plans and got a good look at it. The backup generator is in a new building at the back. It's diesel and that's also where they store the fuel. I know that because the fire assembly point is right on the other side of the building."

"You're brilliant."

"Yeah, I am aren't I!" she paused and smirked. "Plus it was written on the map."

"Okay, let's go and see what Hyodo has found out."

She fiddled with her leggings. "I can't wait to get home, I've got to get out of these pants."

<<<<>>>>

The next day, Dhazi made a trip to the building on his own, scouting around the perimeter fence at the back. He quickly located the building that housed the generator. This was easy to spot as it had an exhaust pipe, and he could hear the soft throb of the engine on tick over. It would be kept running on idle, ready to kick up to full power as soon as the main feed was lost.

That established, he looked for a vantage point. As he walked past, he saw one. The ground to the rear of the building rose slightly and he estimated that he could easily hit the fuel storage drums. He knew the area was covered by CCTV, but there would be a brief moment of confusion as the lights dimmed before the generator was up to full power. He could use this, though realised that he would get no more than three hits before he was spotted.

Attack On The Security Building.

"Ayeka, you go with Hyodo to the hub. I'll hit the security building, I'll know when you've been successful."

The two nodded, this was the agreed plan. They gathered together their petrol bombs, four for the hub, three for the building. It was eight in the evening and already quite dark outside. The plan was for Dhazi to hit his target at eleven-forty-five, just before the midnight shift changeover when the occupants would be tired and reactions slower. All three had long walks ahead, Dhazi shook hands with Hyodo, then turned to Ayeka. They hugged, holding each other tight, there were no words, they both knew how the other felt. Eventually they broke apart.

Dhazi looked at the two. "This is our first strike. What we do today will alter the course of Matrea. It is dangerous, so if either of you don't want to go through with it, say so now, there'll be no shame, I'll understand.

Ayeka cocked her head to one side and gave him one of her looks. "Seriously? You're asking *me* that?"

"Well, it's risky, very risky, and I'm not your commander, I can't order you to do it."

She leant forward and gave him a kiss, then picked up the bag with her two bottles.

"See you later babe."

"See you later Dhazi," sniggered Hyodo, mimicking

Ayeka's voice as he picked up his bag. "I ain't going to give you a kiss though," he said and smirked as the two of them left the flat. Dhazi grabbed his bag and set off in the other direction.

"I didn't see any CCTV," whispered Hyodo as they approached the distribution hub. "There are floodlights, but they didn't look like infrared floods, more like working lights."

She flicked up the hood of her jacket. "Even so, we'd better assume that there are cameras, so let's keep our heads down."

Soon they were at the perimeter fence, it was a cloudless night, and the hub was illuminated by moonlight and small pools of light from bulkhead lamps that appeared to be more for safety than security. Hyodo led the way around the fence to the target, stopping when they were at the closest point.

She looked at the height of the fence and the distance to the transformer. "Easy," she muttered. They listened closely for the sound of human activity, there was none, just the hum of half a million volts surging through the cables.

Hyodo took the bombs out of the bags then pointed at the tubes coming out of the side of the transformer housing.

"We aim for those."

She picked up the first one. "Remember what I said about holding it." Hyodo lit the rag, and she lined up ready to throw. "Ready?"

"I'm ready," he replied as he lit one of his own. "Let's do it."

The first two smashed into the tubes halfway up. There was far more fuel in these than in the test bottle, and sheet of flame covered the side.

"Let's aim higher."

Two more hits saw the whole side burning, the sticky fuel covering every one of the cooling tubes. Within a few seconds they heard a loud crackling from inside the housing.

"It's working already," she gasped. "It must be overheating."

"Yeah, but we've got to leave."

"No, I want to see it go up."

"Err, Ayeka, you'll see it all right, but it won't be safe for us here. They use oil as the coolant, it'll be super-hot now, the transformer will start to melt, the core will short out and it'll go off like a bomb. Trust me, we don't want to be around when that thing goes."

There was a bang as one of the coolant pipes cracked under the pressure; a jet of vapourised oil spurted out, instantly catching fire, blasting out a five metre long flame like a blowtorch.

Hyodo grabbed her arm and pulled her away from the fence. "The coolant's boiling, we've got to go now, we haven't got much time."

They were about a hundred metres away when

there was a much louder bang and a blinding, blue/ white flash, followed by a loud buzzing.

"Run!" he shouted. They had gone another fifty metres when a colossal explosion destroyed the transformer, sending debris clattering to the ground behind them. Ayeka glanced back over her shoulder to see live cables creating brilliant white sparks as they hit the ground, the power of the arcs throwing the broken ends high into the air. Hyodo pulled her around.

"Don't look at it, the ultraviolet light will damage your eyes."

<<<<>>>>

The lights flickered in the security building. The lights around the building dimmed then all the lights went out. Black smoke belched from the generator's exhaust as it began its run up to full power.

"Yes," he whispered, then threw his first bomb. It landed short, but some of the fuel still managed to land on the drums of diesel. The second and third landed square on. It was time to go, he couldn't risk hanging around to see if it worked. He would know.

He hadn't gone far when he heard the first whoomph and the sound of a drum lid landing on the ground. A fraction of a second later there was a much louder sound as a drum burst open, blowing in the side of the generator housing. Burning fuel flooded all around the equipment, melting the insulation on the cables, shorting them out and destroying the generator.

He looked back at the security building, all the lights were out, but he could see the glow from monitors attached to computers that had battery backup systems. He could also see people frantically backing up their work, knowing that they only had minutes in which to do it before the batteries ran out. No data would be lost, but that was not the point of this mission, this operation was a statement, and statement made, he turned and went home.

Ayeka ran to him as he entered the flat. "Did we?"

"Yes, all the lights went out, but I couldn't see how much damage was done."

<<<<>>>

Dhazi woke to find Ayeka getting dressed in the clothes she wore to the station.

"Why are you wearing those?"

"I'm going to find out how much damage you did."

She'd got a look on her face, a look of determination and he knew it was pointless to even try to change her mind.

"Okay, but I thought you said the pants were uncomfortable."

"They are, but hey."

"Be careful."

"What do I need to be careful for? I'm only going to ask if they've..." She dropped into the accent she had used before. "...if, like, they've like, found me 'andbag."

Dhazi rolled out of bed. "I've got to go to work, Hyodo's going to sort out his parents." He chucked the keys to her. "We probably won't be here when you get back."

She chucked the keys back then patted around her hips. "I ain't, like, got no pockets, 'ave I?" then smirked at him. "Gotta stay in character. I'll go and see mum and Dad."

"What, dressed like that?"

"Yeah, I won't tell them, but they'll guess why."

<<<<>>>>

"Me name's Li-ann. I was 'ere, like, a couple of days back about me 'andbag, right? an' I spoke to this well cute bloke. Is he around?"

The desk sergeant pointed to a chair. "I'll see if he's free, wait over there."

This time he was out much quicker. She stood to meet him, thrusting her chest forward as before.

She fiddled with a lock of her hair, looking up at him coquettishly. "You, like, said to come back in a few days. Have you, like, found it yet?"

This time he looked into her eyes instead of down her top. "No," he snapped, then scowled. "We have bigger things to deal with right now. Come back in a couple of weeks."

She pouted, turned and left the building. The detective went to the desk sergeant.

"I don't want to see that silly little bitch ever again," he snarled. "We got firebombed last night and I'm not going to waste my time on some air-head bimbo like her. If she comes back, tell her I'm busy."

Ayeka smiled to herself as she left the building and walked away, the interaction had gone exactly how she thought it would. She glanced over towards the rear of the compound and saw a fire crew damping down around the wrecked remains of the generator. She undid the first button of her already low top, exposing a lot more of her cleavage, then went to the perimeter fence and made big eyes at one of the younger firemen.

"Like, what 'appened 'ere then?"

"Sorry Miss, I'm not allowed to say."

She swayed from side to side fixing her gaze on his eyes, playing the coy flirt. "You can, like, tell me, though, can't cha?" She noticed his eyes drop to her chest.

"Okay, you didn't hear this from me, but there was a firebomb attack last night, they still ain't got power. My mate told me that the distribution hub was hit as well."

"Oh, cool."

His demeanour changed as he realised he'd said too much. "No not cool, now clear off."

She frowned at him. "There ain't no need to talk to me like that, I was only askin'." She turned and stormed off in a huff but smiled to herself. "So easy to manipulate," she muttered.

A truck passed her, on the back was a huge orange box with 'On hire from Matrea Power Generation Services' emblazoned on the side.

An hour later and power restored, inside the police building detective Drumetski was looking through CCTV recordings from the night of the attack. He saw the arc of light from beyond the fence and knew from experience that this was from a petrol bomb. He counted three in total before the stored fuel erupted, causing a white-out, and the screen going blank a couple of moments later as the power to the camera failed. On a hunch he called up CCTV recordings from the same camera over the past few days, noting that in one from two days previously, a person had walked past, briefly stopping in the place where the petrol bombs were thrown from. It was obvious to him what this person had been doing; he got in his car and drove to the distribution hub.

Fire crews had left, electricians had made the area safe and uniformed officers were keeping the curious at bay. He wandered around the blackened mess looking for what he knew would be there – broken glass. It didn't take him long to find it. The transformer feeding the security building was the only one that caught fire, which he thought to be highly unlikely.

He walked to the nearest part of the fence and saw flattened grass and the tracks of two people. He took pictures of everything, collected some of the glass shards, put them in an evidence bag and went back to the office.

He checked the evidence bag into the store, typed up a report of his suspicions, attached the pictures and links to the two recordings, adding a request to be allowed to investigate further.

Calder saw the request and agreed with the suspicions. Detective Drumetski was correct, this was a deliberate, organised attack on the security services. Carefully planned and skilfully executed by multiple individuals so that only the combined security building lost all power, and the general population did not. Whoever was bold enough to carry out an attack so brazen was bound to strike again and it was clear that they would become a direct threat to his rule. The young police detective was right, further investigation was needed.

Calder wasted no time in issuing a series of orders, the first was a DNI order – Do Not Investigate. A follow up order instructed the evidence store to dispose of the glass fragments and delete all records relating to them. A further order to the digital evidence department ordered the deletion of the photos and videos. The final order was for Drumetski to be transferred out of the city and into a regional traffic division hundreds of kilometres away.

<<<<>>>>

The TV was on, but no-one was really paying any attention to the program because it was the evening news. Dhazi and Hyodo were finishing the meal that Ayeka had prepared, while she had gone to wash her hair. She came back into the room rubbing her head with a towel. She looked at Dhazi, he looked at her and his heart fluttered, straggly locks of wet hair were stuck to her face, and she'd splashed a fair bit of water on her clothes.

'How can she stand there like that and still look so good?' he thought to himself.

Hyodo had seen the slightly dreamy expression on Dhazi's face a few times now; the look his friend had whenever he saw his girlfriend. Dhazi was the leader of the nascent rebellion, even though he didn't want to think of himself in that way. He saw himself as just being the first of his generation to try to bring about change. He considered everyone to be equal and to have an equal voice.

Hyodo had no doubt that one day his friend would be the one to finally challenge Calder, but right now Dhazi was getting a bit soppy because Ayeka had just entered the room. He found it cute in a weird sort of way. He also knew that she was the force driving him on.

All three of them had long since dismissed every news article to be at best little more than propaganda and at worst, blatant lies. Dhazi always found the servile and sycophantic attitude towards Calder from the reporters to be verging on obsequious to the point of being offensive to watch. It was plain to him that these people had been put in place by Calder's cronies. He was about to turn the TV off when an article caught his attention.

"...a freak weather event happened last night," came

the cheery voice of the female news presenter. *"Despite there being no thunderstorm, there were two lightning strikes, one at the electricity distribution hub that feeds the East Zone, and one on the combined police and security services building. The transformer at the hub was totally destroyed, but the damage to the building was minimal and power was not lost. Here to discuss this rare event is professor of meteorology Zuko Mayank from the Central University of Matrea."*

"Minimal?" muttered Ayeka as she brushed her hair. "I wouldn't call what I saw as minimal."

"Professor, how common are lightning strikes like these?"

"Well, first let me thank you for having me on. In answer to your question, events like these are far more common than people think..."

Dhazi turned the TV off. "Calder's covering it up, perfect!"

Ayeka frowned. "Isn't that a bad thing? Surely we want everyone to know that it was an attack." Hyodo nodded in agreement.

"No, it's a good thing. It means we've got his attention. I saw the lights go out and you saw the damage to the generator."

Ayeka sat down, instantly switching into serious mode. "Okay, what do we hit next?"

Hyodo put his hand up. "Actually, I don't think we should hit anything else so soon. Remember what the book said? I think we should leave it a little while but in the meantime we explore other means of getting his attention."

Ayeka looked at Dhazi. "Don't you think we should strike while the iron's hot, well, when I say iron, I mean, iron, copper and a little bit of aluminium."

"I think Hyodo's right." Dhazi turned to his friend. "What have you got in mind, Hyodo?"

"We spread the word, but carefully. We talk to kids our age and let them know that it was an attack, but we don't say it was us, because they're bound to talk and that'll spread the word, and actually, that's what we want."

Ayeka nodded to accept his reasoning. "Okay, yeah, good idea. There's plenty of kids fed up with the situation, I hear them whispering about it all the time."

Dhazi sat up straight. "Okay, let's turn the whispers into talk. Sound out kids, get a feel for them. Get talking to ones you trust and find out how far they'd be prepared to go."

"Recruitment?"

"Yep."

Hyodo checked his watch and sighed. "I've got to go, got to sort mum and Dad out. They say they can manage without me, but they can't, they just can't. I'll see you tomorrow."

He left them and Ayeka turned to Dhazi. "Are they really that sick?"

"Yeah."

"What's wrong with them?"

"He'll tell you in his own time."

Hyodo's Parents.

Durie Simu sat wheezing in his wheelchair while his son, Hyodo, looked on, unable to hide his concern. His mother Ji-Soo was just as ill. Both had contracted a disease from breathing in the fumes at the steel works where they had both worked. Hyodo didn't know what the disease was and feared that it was cancer. The only thing he knew was that they needed medication every day or they would die. The letter from the hospital slipped from Durie's hand, just opening the envelope had sapped his strength. "You read it, son, I'm too weak to even hold it now."

Since leaving school, Hyodo had only ever worked part time; having to look after both parents meant that finding a full time job was out of the question. He realised that he'd soon have to quit work altogether as their health was continuing to worsen, and that would mean the family living off their meagre savings and the pitiful handouts from the government. The past two years had been especially tough with their health in obvious decline, and since then it had been difficult getting them to hospital for their regular check-ups and to collect their prescriptions. This was made worse by the rule that all medication had to be collected by the person taking the medication.

In the past, public transport was often crowded with nowhere for them to stand, but public transport was impossible now that they were both in wheelchairs, it simply wasn't set up for wheelchair users. Taxis would refuse to take them, making the false claim that they had some sort of contagion, which was just an excuse to avoid having to help frail people in and out of their cars. Dhazi's father had helped when he could, but they had missed the last appointment.

Hyodo picked up the letter, his heart dropping as he scanned through the text.

"What is it, son?"

"I'll read it to you, Dad."

Hyodo took a deep breath and steeled himself for the delivery of bad news.

Mr and Mrs Simu

You missed your last appointments, and this means that in keeping with hospital policy, you are no longer eligible for free prescriptions. From now on, you must get your prescriptions from your local pharmacy, each will cost you fifty credits.

This decision is final and cannot be challenged.

Hospital administration.

Ji-Soo raised her head wearily. "Durie, that's two hundred credits a week, we can't afford it, what are we going to do?"

Hyodo took hold of his mother's hand. "I'll find the money, mum. I'll think of something."

"No," gasped his father. "There's no point. We have some meds left, we'll use them up and then let nature take its course."

"No Dad, you can't, I have to find a way."

Durie looked at his wife, who nodded her agreement with him. She looked at her son.

"We're so tired of being ill, Hyodo, we're just fed up with it, and it's not fair on you. You've done so much for us, you've sacrificed the best years of your life for us. You have your whole life ahead of you. We can't ask anymore from you. Let us die, and then you'll be free."

Hyodo slumped at his mother's feet, crying. "I can't, I don't want to let you go."

"You have friends, Dhazi and Ayeka will help you, they're good people," she wheezed, the effort of talking exhausting her.

"No, there has to be a way."

Durie summoned all his strength, wheeled himself over and rubbed the back of his son's neck. "It's better this way, we're only putting off the inevitable. We'll take the last of the tablets, that'll give us a few more weeks, then like your mother says, you'll be free to get on with *your* life."

<<<<>>>>

Two weeks had passed and Hyodo was becoming ever more agitated. He'd been sitting with Ayeka in the spare room pouring his heart out to her for the past half-hour. She was shocked, not realising the full extent of the life he was having to lead.

He eventually talked himself out and sat in exhausted silence, just staring at the wall opposite as he contemplated his future. Ayeka went to Dhazi. "He's in a terrible state, he said his mum and Dad have only got a few days to live now. I think it's best that we don't involve him in any plans for the time being, it won't be fair on him."

"Agreed. It's going to be tough for him, he's always been really close to both of them. We're going to have to take him under our wing when they go, because the first thing the council will do is kick him out of the house. I know him, he'll say he'll be okay, but he won't be, and I can't have him sleeping rough on the street. Are you okay with him staying here for a bit?"

"Yeah I'm cool with that, we've got a spare room, and it's the least we can do for him."

Dhazi looked through to Hyodo, sitting staring at the wall. "Poor kid. His mum and Dad met when they working in the armament factory, they were basically poisoned by all the chemicals in the air. He's been doing everything for them for the past couple of years, and I mean everything. What other kid do you know that would carry their mother to the toilet? Or wash her in the shower?" Dhazi scoffed. "It's hardly a positive, but his Dad was so ill, the police didn't ever bother harassing him."

"But nobody else has done anything for them, have they?"

"No, and I feel really bad about it, I feel that I should have done more to help him."

"Well, now's your chance."

"You're right."

Dhazi went through to his friend, sat down and put his arm around him. "Ayeka's just told me everything. You know we'll do anything to help you, just say the word, and when *it* happens, you can come and live here."

Hyodo said nothing, he just threw his arms around Dhazi and sobbed. "I'm sorry," he finally managed to say.

"There's nothing to be sorry for."

<<<<>>>>

It happened much sooner than anyone expected. Just two days after talking to Ayeka, both parents died, and within minutes of each other.

"They knew it was going to happen, and they wanted to be close to each other. I put them side by side. They were holding hands when it happened." Hyodo finally broke down, falling into Dhazi's arms. "I'm sorry," he cried.

"Hyodo, there's nothing to be sorry for, you did everything for them, there has never been a son more dedicated to his family than you. You should be proud of yourself. I know they were proud of you."

Hyodo pulled himself up straight, wiping his eyes with the back of his hand. Ayeka handed him a tissue. "Thank you." He sighed a few times. "Dad was fifty, mum was forty-nine, that's too young to die."

She put her hand on his arm to comfort him. "Are you going to see them one last time? We could come with you if you want."

"Thank you, but no. They were not in good shape when, you know, when they went. The disease had destroyed them, and I want to remember them as they were, not how they became. So I've asked for the coffins to be sealed."

His sadness seemed to ebb, and he lightened up a touch, but getting serious as he thought of all the things he would need to do now. "The doctor has given me the death certificates, I'll have to deal with all the official stuff."

"We'll help you."

"Thanks and I appreciate the offer, but I want to do it, I want it to be the last thing I do for them."

"When's the funeral?" asked Ayeka gently.

"Tomorrow."

Dhazi and Ayeka were taken aback. "So soon?"

"The doctor says that their illness's and decline were well documented, I have the death cert's so there's no need to wait." He shuffled on his feet, embarrassed. "Plus, the undertakers will charge me storage, and I can't afford it. Mum and Dad had nothing, we had to buy the wheelchairs and all the other stuff and there's only just enough for the cremation."

"Can we come?"

"Yes, I'd like that."

<<<<>>>

Apart from the official in charge, the only people at the crematorium were Hyodo, Dhazi and Ayeka. Dhazi didn't ask why there were no relatives present, if Hyodo wanted him to know, he would have told him.

There was no religious element to the proceedings, and both committals were over quickly. The crematorium was state run and designed for swift turnarounds; one coffin was ready to be lowered and the other sat to one side on a conveyer-like system. Ayeka watched Hyodo as the first coffin descended and the second take its place. He seemed to her to be blank, resigned to his future, and no-one wanted to think of the bodies being reduced to ash by the lone worker below as he turned on the gas burners.

"Goodbye mum and Dad, I'll see you again one day," was all Hyodo said. He left and briefly shook hands with the facility manager thanking him, before walking out.

"He's in shock," whispered Dhazi. "He's going to be fragile for a while. I doubt he'll ever be the same."

They went outside to find Hyodo pacing around, deep in thought and seemingly bothered by something.

Ayeka went to him. "Are you waiting for the ashes?"

"No, I've told them that I don't want them. It's morbid,and what would I do with them? People sit with ashes in cupboards for years while they stress about where they should scatter them. Mum and Dad didn't want any of that."

She put her arm around him. "Come on, let's go to the flat, it's your home as well now, and for as long as you need it."

Hyodo seemed deep in thought again, they'd walked a few paces when he stopped and looked at the pair of them. "You're so good to me, mum was right, she said you are good people."

"It's what friends are for."

He turned his head, unwilling to make eye contact.

They both hugged their friend, Ayeka spoke softly to him. "You're emotionally drained, Hyodo, you did so much for them. But it will get better, we'll help you."

He smiled weakly. "Thank you. I hope I never let you down."

Recruitment.

Ayeka frowned, concerned, as she handed over a mug of coffee. "How's your mum doing, Ellie?" The tiny sixteen-year-old hung her head stared at the floor for a few moments.

"Mum's not good, it's been over a month now and she still won't tell me what they did to her, but she's been crying a lot and I saw the marks on her back."

Ayeka reached over and took hold of the girl's hand. "How's your Dad coping?"

"He's traumatised, he blames himself. He was at a club with his drinking buddies, he didn't know until he got home. He says that if he'd been at home they wouldn't have taken her, they'd have taken him."

"Do you know why the special security police took her?"

Ellie scoffed. "Since when do they need a reason?"

"I'm sorry Ellie, that was a bit insensitive of me."

"You don't have to be sorry. It was something to do with the 1027 Committee, whatever that is." Tears welled in Ellie's eyes. "I want to make them feel sorry for what they did to her." She dried her eyes, scowled as she jabbed her finger in the direction of the combined security building. "Shame that lightning strike didn't blow the whole place up and kill the lot of them," she snarled.

Despite Ellie putting on a brave face, the sixteen year old was clearly still desperately upset. Ayeka thought hard about what to say next. Playing on her trauma could be considered emotional abuse, but if there was a right time, then that time was now.

"It wasn't a lightning strike."

Ellie's head snapped up. "What?"

"Lightning wouldn't do that, lightning will always hit the highest bit of metal, so why didn't it strike the pylons?"

"What are you saying? Are you saying that it just blew up? The news said it was lightning."

Ayeka leant forward and lowered her voice. "The news lies, everything they say is a lie." She lowered her voice to a whisper. "I heard there was an attack, a petrol bomb or something was thrown at it. And the strike at the distribution hub? Same thing, pylons all around yet the lightning was supposed to have missed those and hit the smallest thing on the ground."

She looked all around to check if anyone was listening, the only other people in the coffee shop were a few tables away and engrossing in their own conversations. "Someone firebombed it, and whoever did, they must have been working with whoever bombed the security building. It can't have been a coincidence."

"Are you saying that there are people willing to stand up to Calder?"

"Yeah, there must be. Look, I gotta go, look after yourself, and erm, let your mum know that if there's anything I can do for her, just ask. The same goes for you Ellie, just ask, okay?"

Ayeka left the coffee shop struggling with her feelings. Had she just emotionally abused Ellie? Probably, and she felt bad about it.

There had been some rumours of the 1027 Committee starting up again and Ellie's father had been overheard talking about it. An example needed to be made, so their home was raided, and in keeping with standard practice, whoever was in the house was arrested and taken to be interrogated, regardless of who it was. It was a terror tactic designed to strike fear and silence opposition, Ellie's mother had been the only one at home at the time.

The next day, Ayeka was walking past the coffee shop and saw Ellie with her boyfriend, Laro. Ellie beckoned her in. "I asked my Dad about this 1027 Committee, but he wouldn't say what it is."

Ayeka glanced around, nobody seemed to be taking any notice of them. She lowered her voice to a whisper. "Don't ever mention 1027 in public, you never know who's listening and it's dangerous."

"Why?"

"It was an underground organisation dedicated to the overthrow of Calder, it died out a decade or so back, but there's talk of it starting up again."

Laro scowled. "How do we contact them?"

"Why do you want to contact them?"

"My Dad's been roughed up by the cops three times,

and for no reason, my sister and my mum have both been hassled, not as bad as Ellie's mum, but that maybe only a matter of time, and it's only a matter of time before me and Ellie get some. We've been talking, we wanna get involved."

"If it *has* started up again, and that's a big if, then you don't contact them. I reckon they'll have someone checking you out, and when they're happy, they'll contact you. That's the way it would have to be."

Ellie snorted, still angry at what happened to her mother. "Well, I hope they do have someone checking us out, because we want to be involved."

"Look, I'm not saying that it has started up again, but for your own sake, don't ever mention it to anyone."

Ellie and Laro nodded to accept her advice.

Laro looked around to check if anyone was listening, nobody seemed to be taking any notice. "Is it true what Ellie says about that lightning strike? That it wasn't lightning, it was actually an attack?"

"Look, it's just a rumour that I heard, and I don't know how much credibility it's got. It could be true, or it could be just wishful thinking, you know what rumours are like?"

He looked at Ayeka with an intense, eager look in his eyes. "Yeah, but there's always a bit of truth to them, isn't there."

"Maybe there is, maybe there isn't, but just be careful of who you talk to; as I said, you don't know who might be listening. I gotta go, look after yourselves."

Ayeka left them, confident that they would talk to their friends about the attack, but not about the 1027 Committee.

<<<<>>>>

Ayeka tapped Ellie on her shoulder, it had been two days since she had spoken to them in the coffee shop. "I've been following you two for the past twenty minutes, and I followed you for an hour yesterday. You didn't spot me, if you really do want to be involved you'll have to do better than that."

Ellie and Laro stood open mouthed in shock.

"Come on, follow me," ordered Ayeka as she walked on ahead, the two bemused teenagers did what she asked. They got to an abandoned warehouse, Ayeka opened a door and pointed in. They entered to see Dhazi and Hyodo, Ayeka followed them in, shutting the door behind her.

She went to Ellie and put her hands on the teenager's shoulders. "I'm sorry Ellie, but I lied to you. The 1027 Committee doesn't exist anymore, but we do. We attacked the distribution hub and the combined security building. I am the one that has been checking you out. I'm sorry to have deceived you, but it was the only way."

Ellie stood speechless, Laro was excited. "Does that mean we're part of the group? What are we called?"

Dhazi stepped forward. "We're not called anything, giving ourselves a name will give Calder a label to pin on us, a focus, something for his acolytes to crow about on the so-called news channels."

"But are we in the group?"

"Yes. You already know Ayeka, I am Dhazi, and this is Hyodo."

Hyodo nodded to acknowledge them but didn't look at them.

Dhazi put his hand on Hyodo's shoulder and squeezed it gently. "You'll have to forgive Hyodo, he's had a rough time of it recently. It's going to be a while before he'll talk to you. But he's solid."

A little shudder ran through Hyodo's body as he looked away, suppressing a whimper. Dhazi pulled up a box and gestured for the others to do so. They sat in a rough circle.

"Our aims are this: stage one, disruption of services, but only those that will affect the security forces, whether it be the police, riot police or the special security police. We don't do anything that affects the public. We do it in the shadows. Stage two, we build our numbers, kids our age. Stage three, we inspire their parents to join us. Stage four, we move onto the streets. And when there's enough of us, we bring Calder down and end a thousand years of tyranny.

"But all of this will take time, we can't rush any of it. We need to take it slow and steady; if we go in hard too soon, Calder will come back hard on us. So we need to be patient, gradually building it up so by the time Calder realises what is going on, we'll have an army behind us and it'll be too late for him.”

“What do you want us to do?” asked Ellie, a steely determination in her voice.

“Small stuff, a little bit of graffiti, a little bit of vandalism. Nothing big or directly aimed at Calder, no defacing of his images or vandalism of his statues, and not too often, just enough for the right people to notice. We need to make Calder think that the 1027 Committee is active again.”

“Are we the 1027 Committee now?” asked an excited Ellie.

“We have the same aims, but we must never use that name.”

“So what do we do?”

“Spread the word about the attack, but don't talk about it just yet.”

A puzzled Laro put his hand up. “How do we spread the word if we can't talk about it?”

“Are you any good with a spray can?”

“Well, yeah.”

“Just put *‘it wasn't lightning’* on a wall somewhere, but do it small, and nowhere really obvious. Then listen to what other kids say about it, let us know which ones you think are the most interested and we'll do the rest. Do not discuss any of this with anyone else just yet, especially not your parents.”

Ellie and Laro had identified two guys from school

who they knew had parents that had been harassed multiple times. Dano and Raja had both witnessed their fathers being beaten up by the police. Both were bitter about it, and both had spoken openly about trying to find a way to get back at Calder.

Ellie made the first approach, walking confidently to the two as they lolled against a wall in a back alley, smoking. They towered above her and looked down on the tiny girl with a sneering disrespect borne out of their frustration with their circumstances. They were two years older than her and had not been able to find work since leaving school.

She said nothing and just stared them down, looking unblinking at them. Their dismissive arrogant expressions fading slightly to confusion. She pointed further along the wall to the words that Laro had sprayed the previous night. She lobbed a can of spray paint at them.

"If you want to get back at Calder, start putting that on back street walls."

Dano took a long drag on his cigarette, blowing it out slowly. "So how's that going to help, pipsqueak?" he asked dismissively.

"Just do it." She turned and left, walked a few paces, then stopped, tuned and walked back to the bemused pair. "We'll be in touch. And my name's Ellie, not pipsqueak." She turned and walked away leaving the two speechless.

<<<<>>>

The rumours were spreading, even some adults had been heard talking about the graffiti. Most wondered what it meant, others who understood how lightning behaves, realised the significance.

Calder smiled as he looked at the images. He'd spotted the words *'it wasn't lightning'* sprayed on walls in a tunnel under a road and a couple more times on walls in back streets. Now, three weeks later, it had appeared ten more times. As he switched between the images, it was obvious from the different way the letters had been formed that these were the work of more than one individual, two, maybe three, and whoever they were, they were young, probably teenagers. If this was done to get his attention, then it had worked. If it had been done to anger him, it had failed; he would let it continue for a while longer.

The attack on the security building's power supply had impressed him, it had been inventive, well planned, and skilfully executed. Disruption of the security services, followed by acts of petty vandalism was straight out of the 1027 playbook. He knew that because he had a copy of the playbook as well.

Like the book given to Ayeka by her father, the names had been torn out. Though that had never bothered him. It wouldn't have helped him identify whoever instigated these acts. This leader challenging the order was a boy born after the books had been written. A boy from the teacher's class, a boy's name whose name he knew.

He wasn't concerned about the challenge, all of his

sims had predicted it. His plans allowed for it. He would permit further acts of defiance to be made, then make his move. Though an example would need to be made at some point.

<<<<>>>>

A week passed and Ellie had seen the work that the two had done; She reported back to Dhazi and Ayeka, stating that she felt confident about the two, and while Laro wanted to carry on with the graffiti, Ellie was keen to take more direct action. A quick discussion between the three of them led to a plan for a much bolder act, that would confirm the level of commitment of the two potential recruits.

It was time to approach them again. She found them in the alleyway, though this time they weren't so dismissive of her, they had a look that was almost respect.

"Well done," she said flatly. "But we have a test for you, we need to know just how dedicated you will be."

<<<<>>>>

Dano waited on one side of the road with Raja on the other. Ellie waited unto the last moment, then stepped into the road in front of the police car and raised her middle fingers to them. She turned and ran down a side street in the full knowledge that her display of disrespect would not be allowed to go unpunished. The officers both got out of the car to give chase. She quickly ducked into a hole in a wall that was only just big enough for her and heard the frustrated grunts of the men as they realised that they had lost her.

By the time they got back to the car, Dano and Raja had done their work, *'it wasn't lightning'* had been sprayed on both sides of the car. The officers knew the truth of the attack on the combined security building, and both understood the significance of these three words.

Both men looked around frustratedly at the empty street; there were no sounds of footsteps running away, no sounds of triumphant giggling from teenagers. This had been done by people who also knew the truth.

Calder read the report, this was good, it was fitting in nicely with his plan. He didn't care who was leaving the graffiti, but he knew who was behind it, and that was all that mattered. The police were getting agitated, as even the dimmest of officers were aware of the lies about a lightning strike and how dangerous the slogan was becoming. In response they increased stop and search activities and stepped up patrols, all of which served to heighten the animosity between the population and the police.

The police couldn't understand why there were no CCTV recordings from the areas where the slogans had been left. They didn't know that Calder had personally deleted the files. It was all progressing exactly as Calder needed it to

<<<<>>>>

There was one last test that Dano and Raja needed to take. Ellie had suggested it and Dhazi had approved it. It would be a direct attack, but Dhazi, Ayeka and Hyodo would not take part, they needed to be anonymous in case Dano and Raja didn't go through with it. Laro hadn't wanted to take part in the paint attack on the police car but had been emboldened by Ellie's bravery. The four of them had prepared the ground and positioned themselves well, it was a dead end with escape routes that a car couldn't follow. Over the course of a couple of days, Ellie had watched the routines of the police patrols, and in particular the patrol of the car they had vandalised.

She noted that the same two officers were driving the vehicle and that the paint hadn't been completely removed. She could tell by their expressions that they were humiliated by this, and their anger showed. They never saw her, but she would show herself when the time was right.

Today was the day and the time was now. The car was cruising slowly down the road, the two scowling officers scanning the surroundings looking for the girl who had embarrassed them. They didn't have to wait long.

She stepped out into the road directly in front of them.

"Looking for me, losers?" she yelled, then held up both hands, giving them the middle finger, then dived down the side alley. The driver booted the accelerator and turned to follow her, but soon found rubbish bins and junk in the road, forcing him to slow the car. Realising that they couldn't catch her in the car they got out and ran but stopped when they heard a clattering sound behind them. They turned to see rocks raining down on the vehicle.

"Losers!" yelled Ellie as she disappeared down an alleyway. Laro, Dano and Raja, having dented and damaged the car had melted away, but what none of them realised was that a camera had been fitted to the car and it had captured a perfect image of Ellie's face.

Calder studied the image for a while, mulling over the options in his head before settling on the only real option he had. It was time for an example to be made, but he'd let it rest for a while to give these rebels a chance to wallow in their glory. There were other parts of his plan to put in place first. Meanwhile he would have the two officers disciplined for incompetence, and their pay docked to cover the cost of repair to their car. That news should filter through the ranks and make all of his law enforcement officers aware of the cost of failure.

The Bug.

Hyodo sighed as he handed a small box to Dhazi. "Here, I found this when I was going through Dad's old stuff."

Dhazi opened the box, inside was a small circular device that looked a bit like a lightbulb holder and a black box with a USB socket. Also in the box was a USB stick and a power adaptor.

"What is it?"

"It's a listening device." Hyodo sighed then shrugged. "I dunno why Dad had it, but he did, and I thought it might be useful to us at some point." Hyodo's voice was monotone, flat and lifeless. Ayeka had noticed that he didn't make eye contact with them anymore. She put her hand on his shoulder.

"Are you okay, Hyodo?"

"Yeah, well, no, not really. It's hard, you know, going through all their stuff, memories and all that. I can't believe they're gone. Anyway, I had a quick look at this." He held up the circular part. "This is the microphone, it goes between a lightbulb and the fixing, that's where it gets its power. It's got a transmitter, the other box is the receiver, and it records to the USB stick."

Dhazi took the device and studied it. This part was quite shallow, and he felt that it would not alter the position of a bulb enough to be noticed. There was a series of small holes all around the edge and it was obvious that this meant it would pick up sound from all directions.

"Do you know if it works when the bulb isn't on?"

"Yeah, there's a battery in there that gets charged up, so once it's been on for a bit it'll work even if the light's off."

"What's the range? Do you know?"

"Dunno, about ten metres I suppose," he grunted

"I know exactly where I'll place it, thanks Hyodo."

Hyodo's shoulders dropped. "Look, I'm going to go to my room, I'm going to work some things out in my head." He avoided eye contact and Ayeka thought she saw tears in his eyes.

She put her arm around him. "We know it's tough for you right now, but we're here for you."

He swallowed and sighed deeply. "Thank you." He got up and went to his room, closing the door behind him.

Ayeka watched him shuffle away. "Losing his mum and Dad has hit him really hard."

Dhazi shook his head sorrowfully. "Yes it has, and what with our project, I doubt he'll ever be the same Hyodo that I've known for the past eighteen years."

<<<<>>>>

Dhazi got to work early the next day, quickly installing the device in the light above the police officer's table and hid the receiver behind some boxes on a shelf in a cupboard nearby. This was where the cleaning kit was kept, and the owner of the restaurant rarely went in there. It was one of Dhazi's jobs to clear up after everyone had left and this would enable him to retrieve the USB stick every night.

The police officers didn't come in that night, something that everyone was grateful for, though the night was busy, as the lack of the officers meant that customers stayed longer. The manager was happy, and although his workload was a bit hectic, Dhazi was happy too, as there wasn't the constant fear of recognition from the officer who had stopped him and his father all those years ago.

People sat close to the officers' table but not at it, if it had recorded their voices, then it should be enough to prove that the system worked.

Unusually, all the customers had left by quarter past ten, and it was clear that no more would come in, so the manager, pleased with the night's takings, decided to close early. Dhazi cleared up, collected the USB stick and left for home, happy that he could spend a little more time than usual with his girlfriend.

He thought about her all the way home, but this was nothing new, especially since he always had to pass the alley where it all started. He would always glance in and smile when he saw the dumpster that she had been assaulting on that night. He loved her so much, she was the light that brightened the dreary Matrean existence. She was the one driving him on, supporting and encouraging him as they made their plans to make Matrea a better place for everyone. She was the force making him the man he was becoming.

The inevitable question would come soon, he would ask her to marry him, and he knew she would say yes. But that question could wait a little bit longer. He suspected that she really wanted to ask him to marry her, she was that type of girl and he loved her all the more for it.

<<<<>>>>

Ayeka handed Dhazi a drink as he slipped the USB stick into his computer and opened the file from the evening. Conversations had been recorded well, and satisfied, he flopped down on the couch and kicked off his shoes, rubbing his feet from the hours of standing. She pointed to an electrical socket next to the table. "Hyodo replaced a socket today."

"Why?"

"He said it was cracked."

"That's the landlord's job, we should have just reported it and let him sort it out."

"Yeah, I said that, but he said it would probably never get replaced."

"Yeah, that's true."

"Besides, he said he'd got one from when he was clearing out his Dad's stuff."

"Well that was handy, wasn't it?"

"Do you want me to massage your feet?"

"Oh yeah, that'll be nice."

She knelt down in front of him, working her thumbs around the soles of his feet, watching him slowly relax. After a few minutes she looked up at him, an impish grin on her face.

"Hyodo says he's going to stay at his parent's house tonight, he's bothered about someone breaking in. So we are, you know, on our own."

He smirked, he liked it when she was like this, suggestive and playful. "We are indeed on our own."

She looked into his eye, a little hint of lust in hers. "And that is a very comfortable sofa to lay on."

"Yes it is, and I think we should lay on it."

"I think we should have a quick shower first…"

<<<<>>>

"Good work," said Dhazi as Ellie related to him what had happened. Laro was still hyped from his part in the attack.

"Dano and Raja, they really went for it."

Dhazi looked at Ayeka. "It's time we met them."

She nodded her agreement.

"We've got some more kids interested, there's six of them, all with the same experience as us. They've all seen their parent's roughed up and all say they want to find a way to get back at Calder. They've been doing a bit of graffiti, and they scratched up a police van." Ellie swelled with pride. "I'll vouch for them."

"Okay, We'll meet up with all of them, there's a house that we can use, Hyodo will get the details to you."

A week later, Hyodo had met up with the others and led them to the empty house. Laro was with them, and they were waiting for Ellie.

"Where's the other two?" asked Dano.

"Dhazi can't be here, but you'll meet Ayeka, she'll be along later." Hyodo's voice had a slight shake in it, he felt nervous.

Dano looked concerned. "Who's she, you've not mentioned her before?" Laro piped up excitedly. "She's second in command."

"Err, no," said Hyodo with a tremor in his voice. "She's, erm, joint erm, leader." He noticed their confused expressions as they looked at him. "Look, sorry, I've had a bit of a bad time of it recently and I'm not used to sort of being in charge, and I don't really know what to say. I'm sure she won't be long."

"What's going to happen when Ayeka gets here?"

"Well, the first thing is that she's going to thank you for what you've all done, then she's going to explain our aims and then we'll discuss how to move forward."

"Like what?"

"Look, I'm feeling a bit nervous, so let's wait for her."

Ellie was making her way to the house, unaware that a squad van was parked nearby and was waiting for her. She turned a corner and without realising it, was facing them. One of the officers took out a data terminal and called up a 'wanted' file. Her image was the first one displayed.

"Target identified," he barked into his radio.

"Follow, but don't engage, our orders are to wait until she's in the house," came the commander's reply. They waited until she had passed, then quietly got out and followed her. She'd not gone far when she had an uncomfortable feeling and realised that there were people behind her.

She glanced over her shoulder and saw the SSP squad approaching fast. The logical thing to do would have been for her to run and lead them away from the house, but she was young and frightened, and her only thought was to seek safety with the others.

"They're coming!" was all Ellie was able to say as she burst through the door, her eyes wide open in terror.

The Upper East Side.

Present day, the day after the attack.

Dhazi cautiously walked across the street, crossing the invisible dividing line between the two parts of the East Zone, south to north. He would be entering the Upper East side, Lutcher's zone. He was entering without permission from the gang leader and knew that immediately his foot landed on the pavement they would be watching.

In front of him was a dark alley, bordered on both sides by burned out shops, either torched by the owners for the insurance money, or burned out by one of Lutcher's goons. Dhazi avoided looking up at any of the windows, where the gang's lookouts would be stationed. Even if he did look up, he wouldn't see them, they would be away from the window to stay out of sight of Calder's drones, like the one that had been following him, silently tracking him from a hundred metres above. With his heart in his mouth he entered Upper East side and walked as confidently as he could into the darkness. The drone broke off its surveillance as it changed direction, the operator deciding that it was not worth spending any more time on this lone individual.

He'd never been to this part of the upper east side before, but he knew people that had, and it was as bad as they had described. He was about one hundred metres in; there was rubbish in the streets and graffiti on the walls of shops. There was graffiti on walls in Dhazi's part of the zone, but that was often artistic, but the walls here were covered in crude spray-painted images and obscenities. A lot of the shops were burned out, and it seemed that those still trading all had plywood boards across at least one window.

There was a music venue, an old building painted matte black with posters of the latest hot band plastered on the outside. All around the venue were fast food shops, and the vast amount of discarded food cartons bore witness to the success of the gig that had been on the previous night. The pavement here was sticky with hundreds of black circles caused by chewing gum, and where there wasn't gum, there were cigarette butts. He flinched as he caught a movement out of the corner of his eye; a rat was dragging away a half-eaten burger. He passed an alleyway and recoiled from the smell of various bodily products; it was obvious to him that this was a makeshift toilet for concert goers leaving the venue.

He approached a pub, 'The Old Hatmaker' a traditional town pub that was once the heart of the community and named after the industry for which the area was famed No hats were made here now. The lower third of the walls were painted with gloss paint, this was done to make it easier to wash blood away after a fight.

A drunk staggered out and approached, he was the same age as Dhazi, but looked a lot older as alcoholism had already ravaged his young body.

"You ain't got any creds you can lend me have ya, mate? I'll pay you back when I next see you."

"But you're not going to see me again, are you?"

The young man looked disappointed as he swayed back and forth. "No, I ain't." He staggered away to try and find someone else to give him money.

As Dhazi got further in, the atmosphere seemed to change and get a bit better. The street opened out, becoming less claustrophobic. There wasn't so much rubbish and the shops seemed cleaner, and more to the point, intact. But the police, so ubiquitous in his zone sitting in their cars watching people, were noticeable by their absence here.

After nearly an hour he was close to the centre of Lutcher's zone. He entered a shopping mall, in itself not new, but had recently been refurbished. The shops here were new, shiny and modern with glass and stainless steel frontages. Most seemed to be fast fashion and were outlets for surplus stock from major chains that had shops all over Matrea.

There was no hint of vandalism to these shops. Lutcher was not stupid, he knew they would never pay protection money, and would no doubt have heavies of their own who would seek revenge. No, here Lutcher would target the smaller independent outlets, and there were enough nail bars, beauty salons and hairdressers to intimidate, not by vandalism, but by the very real threats of violence.

Dhazi was aware he was being followed and that they were getting closer. It was what he expected, and what he needed. Ahead of him was the exit, once through that door he would be back in one of the crowded old streets that would lead him towards the centre of Lutcher's zone of power.

The automatic doors slid open, and as he left the mall he heard the wailing of two girls with guitars busking their out of tune harmonies to a current pop song through an inadequate amplifier. It was turned up to its maximum and was distorting the vocals, making them shrill and unpleasant, with the girls oblivious to people wincing as they passed by. No doubt they were hoping to be noticed by a talent scout, and no doubt they were having to pay Lutcher for their 'licence' to perform in his zone, either with money or by some other means.

For the first time he saw homeless people on the upper east side streets, all bundled up in their sleeping bags, some in shop doorways with people having to step over them to get inside. This shocked Dhazi, there weren't many homeless people in his part of the zone and those that were there stayed out of sight and mostly in groups in unoccupied buildings..

He was appalled at the callous way shoppers were ignoring them. Lutcher was rich, and he would get genuine respect if he used just a tiny fraction of his money to help these people, not the respect borne out of fear that he received now.

They were getting closer; he estimated four behind him now, a glance in a shop window confirmed it. There were a couple in front, one glanced over his shoulder and glared at Dhazi as they turned down a side road. This was an unspoken instruction for him to follow them. He swallowed hard as he turned left out of the busy street and saw the road empty in front of him, save for the two men. They stopped and turned. He stopped, and looking back over his shoulder he saw that the four tailing him were blocking the exit. There were walls to either side and no way out.

One of the men in front, one who seemed to be some sort of leader, stepped forward and got close. He looked Dhazi up and down, sneering, trying to intimidate him. Dhazi kept his expression neutral, and the man seemed either surprised or irritated that the interloper wasn't scared.

The man got close, almost nose to nose. "This ain't your part of the zone, what are you doing here?"

"I want to speak to Lutcher."

The man stood back and forced a contemptuous laugh. "So you want to speak to Lutcher, do you? A skinny runt like you, what makes you think he wants to hear what you have to say? Now clear off back to your zone and you might not get a kicking."

"He'll want to hear what I have to say."

The man forced a laugh. "Did you hear that lads, he thinks the boss will listen to him."

The other men chuckled sarcastically.

Dhazi ignored them, he summoned all his courage and looked directly into the man's eyes. "He will."

The man got close again, sneering. "Okay, so you tell me what it is, and I'll tell Lutcher," he snarled.

"No. I tell him myself."

The man grabbed Dhazi by the front of his shirt and hauled him close, expecting some sort of fearful reaction, there wasn't one. He held Dhazi for a few moments then released him and took out his phone. Dhazi guessed he was talking to Lutcher. A few moments later the call ended, and the man turned to Dhazi.

"Okay he'll see you."

Dhazi had assumed he would be on the receiving end of some sort of violence, but this interaction had gone better than he had expected and he had relaxed slightly. This was a mistake that taught him a lesson that he would remember. He didn't see the punch coming, the hard blow to his stomach that had him double over. A black bag was slipped over his head, and he was dragged to a waiting van. With his diaphragm in spasm he began to panic and felt that he would not be able to breathe ever again. The bag over his head added to his stress as the loose material was drawn into his mouth every time he tried to take a breath.

Just as he felt that he was about to pass out, his muscles relaxed and he was able to breathe again, though the bag soon filled with his hot humid breath, causing his head to swim.

Despite all this, he was able to judge the vehicle's direction, and it was obvious that they were taking a circuitous route to Lutcher.

He estimated the journey took ten minutes before they stopped and dragged him out. All the time he had been able to hear the two girls' awful singing and now it was loud, so he realised that he had been close to Lutcher's base all along. He was dragged into a building and down some steps into a damp smelling room that sounded big, empty and hard, like metal and concrete. They tied him to a chair and ripped the bag off his head. Sitting opposite him was Lutcher. He stared at Dhazi for a full minute, then got up and walked around the chair that Dhazi was tied into, stopping as he got behind.

"They say you didn't struggle." He leant down and whispered menacingly into Dhazi's ear. "That was probably a good idea." He went back to his chair, drawing it up a little closer and sat opposite, studying him for a bit, seemingly bemused at the audacity of the trespasser.

"I've lost count of the number of people I've killed or have ordered to be killed. You see, when a problem comes my way, I remember what my old man taught me. It was a simple phrase, just four words. He'd say, *'no man, no problem'*. He was always saying it, and I never really understood what it meant until I killed my first 'problem', then all of a sudden it became obvious – if a man becomes a problem, you get rid of the man and the problem goes away." Lutcher raised his hands as if in revelation. "Simple! People are afraid of me now, and with very good reason, but you, I don't know about you. I don't get why a skinny runt like you would risk coming into my zone, demand to talk to me, knowing what *will* happen to you. But you don't seem afraid sitting here with me, which I find confusing, because by now most of my victims are either begging me for mercy or wetting themselves. So you're an odd sort of problem, but a problem none the less."

"I am not afraid of you."

Lutcher cocked his head to one side and let out an amused grunt. "See, there you go. If anyone else had said that I'd have cut off one of their fingers. So why ain't I doing that to you, I wonder? No, you are a mystery to me. What's your name?"

"Dhazi Noran."

"And tell me Dhazi Noran, why did you risk death by coming into my zone without permission."

Dhazi looked him in the eye. "Firstly, I knew you wouldn't kill me, I don't run a gang, at least not yet, so I'm not a threat to you. And secondly, I don't need a permit from you."

Some of Lutcher's men stiffened, no one had dared look at him or speak to him like that before. One picked an electrical cable and raised it ready to lash Dhazi across his back. Lutcher waved him down.

"That is actually true, so why are you here?"

"I wanted to speak to you face to face."

Lutcher laughed but was perplexed by Dhazi's brazen attitude. "And what made you think I would want to speak to you?"

"You're speaking to me now, aren't you?"

Lutcher's face dropped and his men became anxious, this was the look he always had before one of his explosive bursts of temper. Then he relaxed. "I like you, so, what do you want to talk to me about?"

"I'm not going to say anything until you release me."

"I must say, you've got a big pair of balls on you." Lutcher snapped his fingers, and his men released Dhazi, he sat for a moment rubbing his wrists, his expression stern, showing that he wasn't intimidated.

Lutcher made rapid circles with his fingers. "Come on, what is it? I'm not known for my patience."

"I want you to make peace with Orlo."

There was stunned silence for a moment.

"Do what!" gasped Lutcher. His men became agitated, unsure of how he was going to react.

"I said, I want you to make peace with Orlo."

Lutcher roared with laughter, his men nervously joined in. Dhazi sat staring at him, his expression stern. Gradually Lutcher stopped then looked him quizzically.

"You want me to make peace with the boss of the South side, my enemy?"

"Yes, it's important."

"You're actually serious, aren't you?"

"Yes I am."

Lutcher leant forward, baring his teeth. "I have killed men for less than that."

"You're not going to kill me."

Lutcher scowled. "Don't count on it!"

Unfazed by the threat, Dhazi continued to look him in the eye. "Why would you kill me when I have information that could help you."

"I don't need your help." Lutcher snapped his fingers at his men. "Get him out of here."

Hands grabbed Dhazi hauling him to his feet, marching him towards the door. He turned and looked back at the gang boss.

"At two-thirty tomorrow afternoon, fifty squads of the SSP will enter your zone with orders to kill you."

Lutcher snapped his fingers again and waved his men back. They shoved him back in the chair; Lutcher got close. "Tell me more," he demanded.

"Calder thinks people are getting too powerful and he wants to make some examples, he's hit one group already."

"Yeah I heard about that, a load of kids were killed."

"Yes, and a couple of them were my friends, they were kids who wanted to strike out against Calder but Calder isn't finished. I didn't know about yesterday's attack, but I do know that he wants to make an example of you. Riot police will surround the area and block off all escape routes, then the special security police squads will move in. They'll go in every building and kill anyone that refuses to say where you are until they find you. There'll be no negotiation, they'll not take you prisoner, you'll just be shot. Your body will not be dumped in the street as an example and a warning to others of the consequences of getting too powerful. Because even though you have ruled by fear, such an action might make you become some sort of a folk hero." Dhazi paused and fixed a knowing look on the gang boss, staring deep into his eyes. "The only advantage you have is that they don't know what you look like." He spoke slowly to emphasises his point. Lutcher sensed that Dhazi was sending a message, a message that he understood, but none of his men did.

The gang boss hid his shock but was inclined to believe it. There was something about Dhazi's confidence that impressed him. "How do you know all this?"

"I have a way of getting information."

"If you're setting me up, I will personally kill you," snarled Lutcher, though in the back of his mind something stirred, Dhazi had a quality that he had never seen before.

Dhazi reached into his pocket and took out a piece of paper. "This is my home address I'll be there tomorrow evening. If you are not raided, then come to my home and kill me. I won't stop you."

He handed the paper to Lutcher who sat stunned, speechless at this young man's courage.

Dhazi stood up. "Now you know where I live, so I want your men to take me home now."

"Why are you doing this?"

"Something's coming and it's bigger than you!"

<<<<>>>>

At precisely two-thirty, fifty fast response armoured personal carriers thundered into Lutcher's zone, ten vehicles through each of the five main routes into the area. Riot police jumped out of following vans to block the roads and seal off all main and secondary escape routes. The SSP squads got out of their vehicles and calmly started a systematic search of the zone, gradually working their way towards the centre.

Lutcher sat in his underground headquarters, he could hear the rattle of gunfire and the sound of stun grenades detonating. It was getting close. The four men of his inner circle, his most trusted lieutenants looked worried, they had plenty of guns and ammunition, but the weapons and tactics of the special security police were in a different class.

Lutcher contemplated his options, he estimated that it would now be less than fifteen minutes before they were found.

He stood up dramatically, then took off his jacket. "Send out the new guys, three of you, go with them, Kural, you stay, I need you here with me."

The men immediately turned and left.

Kural turned to Lutcher. "They won't be able to repel them boss, we just don't have the firepower. They'll be slaughtered."

"It will give us time."

"Time for what?"

"Time to get away." He took his jacket and handed it to Kural. "Put this on."

Though puzzled, Kural did what he was told, but didn't see Lutcher step behind him and draw his pistol. He quickly raised the gun to Kural's temple and fired one shot. Lutcher placed the gun in the dead man's hand then locked the door, drawing the heavy bolts across top and bottom. It wouldn't hold them forever, but it would give him a few more minutes.

That done, he headed for the secret entrance in the darkest corner of the room. The door that looked like just another metal panel on the wall. He had always known that this day would come, the day when Calder would send his troops to kill him. Either that or one day he would be deposed and killed by one of his own men, someone close to him, and he'd always known that it would be Kural who would assassinate him and take over.

The heavy steel door was stiff, he expected that, but he got it open and climbed through. Once inside, he pulled the door shut, then took the bolts he had placed there years before and spun them through holes and into the door. He took a wrench and tightened them, securing the door from the inside. Now to wait. He didn't have to wait long, there was a louvred grille in the door, through which he could hear, but not see what was going on. He heard the breaching charge blast a hole through the door, followed by the detonation of a stun grenade then yelling that abruptly stopped. Voices carried confusion and disappointment, then more yelling.

The four-man squad stood looking down at the body.

"He took the coward's way out," grunted one.

"Saved us a job," grunted another.

Mission commander Yadav entered the room and looked at the corpse. "We have to know if it's him, get the woman."

In the secret room, Lutcher heard what was said and put his head in his hands, knowing what was going to happen.

The bloodied and injured Sakami, Lutcher's wife, was dragged in. They had guessed she was his wife and had beaten her until she revealed the location of the basement. She gasped as she saw the body lying in the pool of blood, still holding the pistol, and wearing the jacket she had made for her husband. The commander saw this as a good sign.

"Is that Lutcher?" he demanded.

"I'm not going to help you," she snarled defiantly, and got the butt of an assault rifle to the side of her face, knocking her to the ground. Lutcher heard his wife's cry but stayed silent.

The commander grabbed her by the hair, pulled her to her knees then grabbed her head, turning her face to the dead body, while one of his men rolled the corpse's head to face her, a head that had a large part of the left side missing. She said nothing, until she heard the click of a pistol being cocked and felt its muzzle on the back of her head.

"I will ask you again, is that Lutcher?"

"It is Lutcher."

"Thank you."

A single shot ended her life.

She'd known it wasn't her husband as soon as she saw the gun in his right hand; Lutcher was left handed. But she had also known that she would not be leaving the room alive. Bile rose in his mouth and anguish filled him as he heard his wife's lifeless body slump to the floor.

Lutcher heard Yadav call in the missions' success and heard the laughter of the squad as they left. An hour passed and there were no more sounds of death. Lutcher undid the bolts, entered the room and went to the body of his wife. She had sacrificed herself for him and he was filled with an immense feeling of loss. He could have given himself up and that might have saved her, but the calculation he had made while hiding was that they would have killed her anyway. He was humbled by her strength, and for the first time in his life he knew what it was to be a coward. It was time to go, he took Kural's jacket and left the room, making his way upstairs, he would return later to collect and bury his wife.

Five hours had passed since the start of the operation and mopping up had been completed. He flicked the hood up over his head and hunched down as he entered the street. All of the SSP squads were getting ready to leave, he saw them in the distance and was sickened as he heard them laughing and joking, slapping congratulations on the squad that believed they had found his body. He heard the distinctive voice of the commander who had shot his wife, he would remember that voice. Looking, but being careful to not be seen looking, he studied the man's face, memorising it.

"One day," he muttered under his breath as he skulked away.

Rain started, heavy drenching rain that even the most hardened troops didn't want to be out in. They quickly got in their personnel carriers and left. Within minutes, red tinged streams were flowing down the sides of the road. Lutcher saw the bodies in the streets, bodies of civilians, but no bodies of the squad members. They could have been hurt and taken away by their own men, but in his heart he knew that no SSP men had been injured, let alone killed. It had been a one-sided massacre. He had bullied these people, extorted, violated, and murdered them, but they were *his* people and he felt different now. He took the piece of paper Dhazi gave him and made his way to the Lower East side.

Dhazi opened the door to a bedraggled Lutcher. "They killed my wife," he gasped as he slowly sank to his knees.

Lutcher's Change.

Dhazi looked at Lutcher as he handed the gang boss a mug of coffee, a man with a different demeanour than he had when he last saw him.

"Thank you," he muttered as he took the coffee and sat thinking.

"Who did you sacrifice?" asked Dhazi knowingly.

"Kural." He shrugged with more than a hint of self-contempt. "He was my first lieutenant, he'd been with me from the start. We'd been working scams together since we were eight, we'd been taking money from people for sixteen years, but I knew he would move against me one day, and soon, I could sense it. I sent my newest foot soldiers out to face the squads, cannon fodder to give me time to hide. The three other men you saw, they're dead, and I'd sent my best men out of the area, so they are still available to me. Though I don't know what I'm going to do now, everything's changed."

"Will you make peace with Orlo?"

Lutcher swirled his coffee, staring into it, deep in thought. "It will be difficult, we've been fighting for so long…"

"And for what?" interrupted Dhazi.

Lutcher shrugged. "For nothing really, we just fought because we could."

"No. You fought because that's what Calder wanted you to do, you continue to fight because that's what Calder wants you to do. You are playing the game that he made up. I'll talk to Orlo, I'll be your envoy, I'll be independent, not part of your gang."

"He'll kill you."

"You didn't kill me."

"I'll come with you."

"No, you'll stay here, I'll go alone."

Lutcher half laughed, but without humour. "Ten hours ago I'd have slit the throat of anyone who spoke to me like that, and now look at me, I'm taking orders from a weedy little runt." A tear dripped into his coffee. "The bastards killed my wife."

Dhazi reached over and put his hand on Lutcher's shoulder, the man instantly broke down, crying.

"You will have your revenge, Lutcher, I promise you that."

Lutcher looked up, unable to hide his anguish. "Please don't tell anyone you saw me like this."

"I won't, you have my word on that."

Lutcher dried his eyes and regained his composure. "What is this thing that is coming?"

"If we all pull together, if you make peace with Orlo and join forces, we can defeat Calder, we can end this, we can give the people of Matrea a future. He's the reason we have these crappy lives, he's the reason why you fight Orlo."

Lutcher looked up at Dhazi with a look that was different, it was a look of respect. "My men are at your disposal."

"This will not be a swift campaign, it will take time, so you will have to be patient. But I will make you this promise, you *will* get the chance to avenge your wife."

"I will wait, because revenge matures with time, it gets stronger, more sophisticated and is so much more satisfying when it happens."

Meeting Orlo.

Dhazi walked onto the bridge, stopping just north of the centre line. He knew he was being watched by someone whose job was to look out for anyone crossing the footbridge. Someone that could be associated with Lutcher. Dhazi held a piece of paper aloft for a few moments, then reached over to the south side of the dividing line, placed the note down then turned and walked back. He didn't look back, he didn't need to, he knew that the watcher would already have run onto the bridge to retrieve the note.

Twenty-four hours later.

Dhazi saw the spotter as soon as he stepped onto the bridge that would lead him into the South Zone. As he crossed the mid-point, whoever it was on the far side got on a motorbike and sped away. A couple of minutes later a large car with blacked out windows pulled up. He stepped off the bridge and was firmly in Orlo's territory. He would have to pass the car and had no doubt who had sent it.

The message had clearly got through, and there was no way they could mistake Dhazi for one of Lutcher's men, so he felt relatively safe. Even so, his heart was in his throat as he approached the vehicle.

He was ten metres away from it when the thick set driver-cum-bodyguard got out of the front and held the back door open

"Get in," he snarled.

"Do I have a choice?"

"No! Put your arms out, I gotta check you."

Dhazi stood by the car door and raised his arms to allow the man to frisk him. The driver then took a small box, pulled an aerial out and waved it all around Dhazi's body.

"He's clean, no radio or recording device either," he grunted to the person in the car. A hand beckoned Dhazi in. The heavy got in the front. The driver started the car and pulled away. Dhazi was sitting in the back, next to him was a man probably about the same age as him. This man had long, straight white hair, pale skin, piercing blue eyes and a slightly androgenous look, almost feminine.

"I am Orlo. When you look like I do you tend to stand out, you tend to be a target. I had to learn at a very early age to look out for myself, and what I learned was to make people fear me, and most people fear violence. It is a natural and wholly understandable fear, so I used violence, it gave me power. The more people that feared me, the more powerful I became, and it is a well-known aspect of human psychology that people are drawn to those that have power. I drew people to me, and it wasn't long before I didn't need to be physical with anyone, just my presence was enough, and if it wasn't, I had plenty of people willing to do that for me. Indeed, they now see it as an honour. But that's enough about me, what about you? You intrigue me, you are not intimidated by me, instead you seem to have a confidence about you. So tell me, why are you here?"

"I want you to make peace with Lutcher."

The man in front tensed. Orlo showed no reaction, instead he raised his hands and tapped his fingertips together then turned and fixed a stare into Dhazi's eyes. "And why should I do that?"

"Lutcher is no threat to you, and he never has been. He has no territorial designs on the south."

Dhazi knew he had to pick his next words with extreme care, if he got this wrong then all-out war between the two gangs could break out, and that would suit Calder very nicely. Though Orlo seemed receptive and appeared to be anticipating more.

"If you do have ideas about spreading your influence in the north, then now is the time to do it, Lutcher has been weakened."

A strange air came over Orlo, he frowned then hung his head just a fraction and was silent for a moment.

"I heard about the raid, and I know what happened to Lutcher's wife. That was wrong, despicable. I have no qualms in dealing with Lutcher's men, and I would have no issue in personally killing Lutcher. But we leave the women alone." He paused, he knew how much Sakami meant to Lutcher and how much his wife meant to him. He wondered how he would feel if his wife was killed by Calder's men. "It must have been hard on him."

"It was, and it still is. She sacrificed herself to save him."

This seemed to affect Orlo, he was silent for

a moment. "That was... admirable," he eventually muttered. "Tell Lutcher that I too grieve for his loss, and as such, I am prepared to make a temporary truce."

"Temporary? Why not make it permanent?"

Orlo's eyes narrowed and the man in front seemed to be reaching for something. Dhazi held his nerve, refusing to be intimidated. The man produced a gun and levelled it at him. Orlo waved him down and relaxed. "Keep talking."

"Why do you fight Lutcher?"

Orlo went to speak, but Dhazi cut him off. "You fight because you always have done, and for no other reason, and that's what Calder wants; he's using you, just like he uses everyone. The tech companies in the North-West Zone employ a lot of people from the south. So what if I told you that Calder is going to make a few of them fail. It's part of his plan to let the north-west stagnate. Loads of people will be made redundant, and that will directly affect your income."

"How can you possibly know that?" snapped Orlo, his expression making it clear that he fully realised the impact of people not having money to spend in the places that he took money from.

Dhazi stared into Orlo's eyes, this was risky, as the man seemed a bit agitated now. But Dhazi felt confident and guessed that Orlo was the kind of person who actually respected people who stood up to him. "I'm not going to tell you. But what I am going to tell you is that Calder will use the unemployment to sow unrest. He is banking on new gangs forming, gangs that will defy you and will try to take over your territory. He wants to destabilise the south. He wants you to stay as the main gang leader, but with reduced power so you'll be constantly challenged."

Orlo sat processing what he had just heard, shocked at the possibility of opposition to his rule.

"If what you say is true then…"

"It is." Dhazi interrupted.

"*IF* what you say is true," snapped Orlo. "How do I stop it?"

"*You* don't stop it, *we* stop it."

"What!"

"The first step is for you to make peace with Lutcher. I will arrange a meeting, it will just be you, me and him."

"It could be a trap. I will want my men with me."

"You believe it's a trap because you've been fighting for so long you've lost the ability to trust anyone. So, no. You come alone or not at all, you have to trust me."

"How do I know I can trust you?"

"You don't. You'll have to rely on your instinct."

"If it is a trap, my men will hunt you down and you will die a horrible death."

The man in front looked at Orlo in the mirror, expecting an instruction, and silently raised his pistol.

Dhazi remained still, unimpressed and

inscrutable.

"Take our guest back to the bridge," came the order that the driver didn't expect.

There was silence as they made their way back, Orlo was processing the information, and Dhazi chose not to say anything else, believing that his silence would say it for him. Instead he looked straight ahead, hoping the anxiety of the past fifteen minutes wouldn't show.

They were soon back at the bridge, Dhazi got out of the car, leaning back in to Orlo, who now had a different attitude to when he got in. "I'll be on the centre line of the bridge tomorrow at midday. I'll expect your answer then." The gang boss said nothing, but he didn't say no.

He shut the door and started to walk away, wondering if he would get a blow to the back of the head and get dragged back to the car, taken somewhere and beaten. But a blow didn't come. Only when he crossed over the centreline of the bridge did he relax. He hadn't expected violence, as he knew that Orlo's methods were much more subtle, relying on psychological menace rather than physical menace. But he hadn't been one hundred percent sure and having to keep his cool during the interaction with the gang boss had been the most stressful thing he had ever done.

His heart rate was back to normal by the time he reached the other side and was on his home ground. Ayeka and Lutcher were there waiting for him.

"Well?" grunted Lutcher. "Is he going to go for it?"

"I'll know tomorrow at noon."

Ayeka resisted the urge to put her arm around Dhazi as they walked away, she knew it would remind Lutcher of Sakami, and despite his outward appearances, he was still feeling her loss and grieving for her.

<<<<>>>>

There were twenty-one lampposts on the bridge, number eleven was exactly in the middle, and Dhazi was standing just to the north of it.

He checked the time, it was five minutes to twelve. He knew he was being watched, as the man with binoculars thirty-five metres away on the south side was making no attempt to hide. If this was to intimidate him, it failed, and he needed to let the man know that. So he turned and looked directly at the man, keeping his expression stern and serious. He stayed like that for a while, then turned back, disinterested, but out of the corner of his eye he watched as the man went to a car and spoke to someone. Another man got out and started up the bridge.

Dhazi didn't turn to meet the man, he stayed leaning against the iron railing, casually looking out over the river. The man stopped just to the south of the post, and he too looked out casually.

"My name is Di-aal, I am Orlo's second in command, I speak for him. I also kill for him, a knife is my preferred way, there's something about a knife that's more satisfying than a gun. With a gun, you can be a hundred metres from your target, and you'd just see them drop, you might not even hear anything. With a knife, it's so much more personal, you see their fear, you feel their fear, you hear the gasp as they realise that they are about to die. Sometimes I embrace my victim so that I can feel their life slipping away. I would consider it an honour to push my blade into your heart."

Dhazi ignored the bluster from this man who was using it to cover his insecurities.

A flock of birds took flight from the north edge and flew to the south bank, other birds there ignored them as they all pecked in the mud for worms, he nodded towards them.

"Humans are supposed to be smarter than animals, but you don't see them killing each other, do you?"

Di-aal huffed, unimpressed and seemingly a bit annoyed that Dhazi wasn't intimidated by him.

"I'm guessing the answer's yes."

"When?" grunted Di-aal.

"Tonight, eight o'clock."

"Where?"

Dhazi pointed over to a small island that sat in the middle of the river. It was little more than a flat open space that was occasionally used by fishermen. It had a jetty on either side and was perfect for Dhazi's plan.

"There. It's exactly half-way." Then he pointed to

each bank of the river. "Tell your boss that him and Lutcher will each take a boat and approach from their own side and will come alone. I will already be there, if I see anyone else in the boats, the deal's off. No cameras, phones, no recording devices and no weapons. The only tech allowed will be scanners, Orlo brings his, Lutcher brings his. They'll each wait on either side of the island while I scan them. Tell Orlo that any deviation from this and the deal's off and they can both go back to killing each other's men and play the game that Calder wants."

He had watched the man stiffen as he had laid down the rules for the meeting, and could almost feel an anger growing, but he had to come across as firm, anything less would be seen as weakness. And he also knew that despite his earlier bluster, Di-aal wouldn't do anything.

"Orlo doesn't like being dictated to," he snarled.

"Well that's a shame, isn't it?"

"You've got some guts, but if this is any sort of trick…" he turned to Dhazi, a dark menace in his eyes. "…I will find you and kill you… slowly."

"Tonight, eight o'clock. Tell him to be there." Dhazi turned and walked back to the north side, leaving Orlo's man speechless.

"Slow down, heart," Dhazi muttered to himself as he put his hand to his chest and felt the thumping.

<<<<>>>>

The two implacable enemies stood in silence five

metres apart. They had been staring each other down, each trying to gauge the other's intentions.

Dhazi was nervous but was trying hard not to show it. If this meeting failed there could be war between these two men, then there would be no stopping Calder.

Orlo was the first to break eye contact, he bowed his head slightly. "It was with great sadness that I learned of Sakami's death, please accept my condolences."

Lutcher flinched and his shoulders dropped at the mention of his wife's name. He swallowed hard, it was the last thing he expected to hear.

Emotion stole his voice. "Thank you," he whispered, then pulled himself up straight.

"Listen to what Dhazi has to say. It makes sense.

Orlo turned to face Dhazi. "I'm listening."

"You fight each other because you always have, and only because that's what your fathers did, but they didn't know why either, but I'll tell you why. You fight each other because that's what Calder wants. He creates situations to divide and conquer. While you're sitting in your zones brooding about each other, you are blind to the fact that you are doing exactly what he wants. But my question to you is this: what do *you* want?"

Orlo had tried to remain inscrutable, but Dhazi detected the slightest flinch, and it was clear that Orlo didn't actually know what he ultimately wanted.

"Do you have money?"

"Yes."

"How much?"

"A great deal."

"When money is not a problem, then acquisition of power becomes the driver of ambition. Do you have power?"

"Yes."

"Do you seek territorial gains north of the river?"

"No."

"Then look around you, see the miserable lives of the people, what is the point of having total power over a crushed society? You could use your power to make people's lives better, the power you'd get back would be from respect, not fear."

Orlo's eyes narrowed, and there was a moment when Dhazi thought he was going to speak, but he remained silent, his mind running through options and scenarios.

"Lutcher has no desire for territory on your side of the river. So end your war with him and stop your intimidation of the people in the south."

Lutcher stepped forward. "Whatever you decide to do, I give you my word that my men will not attack yours."

Again, Dhazi noticed a slight flinch from Orlo.

"Unite with us, Orlo, and with our combined strength, we can take down Calder."

Orlo turned, looking back over his shoulder to the south bank, he stared at his territory for a few moments, shaking his head slightly.

"I meant what I said about my men." Lutcher's voice was softer now, lacking the harsh aggressive edge of before. "I lost men in the raid, and I am weaker. You would be able to take my territory, and should you decide to do that, then I will not oppose you."

Orlo turned to face them, nodding slightly to accept what Lutcher had said. Then he looked to the ground, shaking his head.

"These things that you ask, they are difficult."

"I know," said Dhazi. "So I propose that before we join forces, we will need to meet a few more times, but we can't meet here."

"Where do you propose?"

"We meet in a safe house in each other's territory. I know it will be difficult for both of you, but there can be no more neutral ground, and no places that are off-limits to anyone." He looked hard at the two. "There is only one Matrea and it is ours, not Calder's."

Both Lutcher and Orlo stiffened, Lutcher especially so, as Dhazi had not shared this aspect with him.

"I know that it will be hard and will take work. Time will be needed to build trust, but we have to stop playing Calder's game and putting an end to the north/south divide will be the first and most important step. We won't need to take any direct action just yet, the simple fact that the fighting has stopped will be enough to concern Calder. But there won't be anything he can do directly, even he can't have people harassed for not fighting, so he will try to sow dissent in the ranks and that is something that you two will need to watch out for."

Orlo raised his head proudly. "My men are loyal, they will do as I command."

Lutcher straightened up and pulled his shoulders back. "As are mine."

Orlo looked at Lutcher and Dhazi. "I will join you."

Orlo was the first to offer his hand in friendship, Lutcher didn't hesitate to take it, pulling Orlo close and hugging him. "Thank you for what you said about Sakami," he whispered.

"I felt your loss. It made me think about all the deaths and the damage that we have done to each other. It saddens me to think it is the loss of your loved one that has brought us here tonight," Orlo whispered back.

They released and Lutcher stepped back. "As a mark of good faith, and a sign of my trust in you, the next meeting will be on your ground, and I will not have my men with me, only Dhazi."

"Then I will repay this trust with a visit to your ground. I too will come alone."

Dhazi sensed a need to set the record, to start them off on the right path. "After the second meeting, we must no longer refer to north and south being one person's ground. It is to be referred to simply as the north zone or south zone, with free travel between both for all. Agreed?"

"Agreed."

"We cannot communicate with phones they are all monitored. Messages will be left on the bridge to start off with and once we have established full trust in each other, then meetings will be easier. Calder will know that former gang members are moving between north and south, so we will need to set up safe houses for meetings."

They shook hands, a three-way handshake that all knew to be genuine. Orlo nodded respectfully to Lutcher, who did the same, then they turned and went back to their zones.

Lutcher scowled slightly at Dhazi as they walked away. "You didn't tell me about going to each other's territory, why not?"

"I needed you to be as surprised as Orlo, if you weren't then he could have suspected that a future meeting would be a trap. I meant what I said, no neutral ground, nowhere is off limits. This is our Matrea!"

Lutcher And Orlo's First Meeting.

Dhazi and Lutcher crossed the bridge, Dhazi's heart was pounding in his chest, and if Lutcher was stressed, he wasn't showing it. Though Lutcher was apprehensive, this was the first time he had entered the south without a weapon.

Waiting for them was a car with blacked out windows. Dhazi tensed as they got close. The door opened Di-aal got out and opened the rear door.

"I have been told not to frisk you," he snarled as the two men got in. This was the most dangerous situation that Dhazi had ever been in. Orlo could have changed his mind, but Dhazi felt that was unlikely, though not impossible. They had no weapons but didn't know if Di-aal or the driver had. They had no control over the destination, they could be driven to a killing field somewhere.

On the way to the bridge, Dhazi had voiced his concerns about bags being placed over their heads. Lutcher, more in tune to the mentality of a gang boss, pointed out that in this instance, a bag would mean they would be taken to a remote spot to be killed.

"That's what I would have done," he said, with just a hint of shame.

No bags were placed on their heads and both men relaxed as far as the situation would allow.

After about twenty minutes, the car pulled up outside a mansion. Orlo was waiting outside for them. He extended the hand of friendship to both men; no-one saw the sneer of disgust on Di-aal's face.

He led them through the lobby into an elegant drawing room. In the middle was a round table and three chairs. On the walls were paintings, Orlo noticed Dhazi looking at them.

"I like to paint, these are all by me."

"They're very good."

"Thank you. I like to paint landscapes, but if you notice, there are no birds in the sky in any of my paintings. Since meeting you I have realised that there is a reason I never paint birds. Birds in flight represent freedom, the freedom to go anywhere at any time. It was my subconscious telling me that we are not free, even I am not free."

Lutcher studied the paintings, admiring the brush work that close up was just a blob of paint, but at a distance came to life as a shimmer of light on a river.

"I've never been one for art, but I like these. Where is this?"

"It's from my imagination, and I guess that the tranquillity is just another subliminal message from my psyche telling me that what I desire is peace."

Orlo gestured to the chairs. "Shall we begin?"

All three sat down. Orlo cleared his throat. "We will be alone in this room and will retire to another room for coffee later." He paused and composed himself. "Thank you for coming, I realise that it must have been stressful for you. But rest assured, I have told my men that there are to be no weapons today.

"I have thought a lot about your words, Dhazi. I have thought about my position. I have thought about Lutcher and his situation, and it is clear to me that we must unite..."

The door opened and in walked Di-aal with two other men, their expressions stern, their hands ready to draw their knives. Lutcher and Dhazi stiffened, Lutcher glared at Orlo, who looked genuinely surprised.

"You said we would be alone," snarled Lutcher.

Orlo remained calm and stood up. "We were supposed to be."

Lutcher went to stand, but Dhazi sensed something in Orlo's demeanour and waved him down. Orlo went to Di-aal.

"I said no weapons. Why have you brought yours?" he asked calmly.

"Lutcher is our enemy." Di-aal pointed angrily at Dhazi. "This is a trick by him. We must kill them both now, and then we win." He went to take a step forward, Orlo put his hand up to stop him.

Orlo turned to Lutcher and Dhazi. "Di-aal is my number two, he will take my place should I no longer be around." He turned back to his man. "Give me your knife."

Lutcher tensed, getting ready for an altercation, but again, Dhazi sensed something, and for some reason didn't perceive any danger.

Di-aal drew the weapon and handed it to his boss. Orlo raised his left hand, showing his palm to Lutcher and Dhazi.

"I am a man of my word, and I will tell you now that the only blood spilled today will be mine."

Orlo drew the blade across his palm, the skin paring open under the razor sharp metal. He did not flinch, did not react, but remained calm as his blood flowed freely, dripping onto the floor. Lutcher nodded his respect.

"The only blood spilled today will be mine... and Di-aal's."

Before Di-aal could react, Orlo spun around and slashed the blade across his throat cutting deep into his flesh. Blood sprayed from the man's mouth as he slumped to the floor.

"I SAID NO WEAPONS," screamed Orlo at the dying man, then slammed the blade into Di-aal's chest over and over again. He glared at the two other men, a manic look in his eyes.

"It is not wise to defy me. Now get this filth out of my sight and bring me a bandage."

Apart from Orlo's voice, Di-aal's death had been almost silent. The two men dragged the body out as Orlo went back to the table, frowning at the blood on his immaculate jacket, and the smear of blood across the parquet floor.

He sat for a moment, eyes closed, calming himself.

"Where possible I prefer to cut throats, blood flows down into the lungs and prevents the victim from screaming. I don't like to hear screaming, it upsets me." Orlo bowed his head slightly. "I apologise for the actions of my men, it was... disrespectful. Rest assured that the other two will not see another sunrise. Now, where were we?"

Though shocked at the idea of Orlo killing the other two men, Dhazi did not attempt to question it. These were Orlo's men and how he maintained control was his way, though it was something that Dhazi realised that he would need to change if they were to be successful against Calder.

Four hours later the meeting was concluded to the satisfaction of all parties, a rough framework for collaboration was in place and it was time to arrange another meeting.

"I have a place where we can meet." Lutcher cringed slightly as he spoke. "It is not as pleasant as here, but it is safe. As you are no doubt aware, conditions north of the river are a bit harsher than in the south."

"Then that is something we will change," replied Orlo, emphatically.

The Second Meeting.

Orlo passed lamppost eleven and was now in the northern zone, a place where he had never been before. As he continued on he noticed a change in the vibe, the north side of the river was where the old docks had been. The docks were long gone, along with the jobs they used to provide, but the buildings remained. Dilapidated warehouses and rusty cranes lined the abandoned wharf.

Half-hearted efforts had been made to turn some of the buildings into enterprise zones and bring some jobs back to the area, but everyone knew that Calder would never let these become anything meaningful. Industries that provided jobs were in the north and northwest, and higher than average unemployment in the upper and lower east side zones suited Calder's plans.

Ahead, Orlo saw Dhazi, Lutcher and a woman standing by a car. As he approached, Lutcher stepped forward and shook his hand, Orlo's grip firm and friendly. Dhazi followed, also receiving a firm handshake, he then gestured to Ayeka.

"This is Ayeka, my partner."

Orlo nodded respectfully as he shook her hand, his grip less forceful. He looked in her eyes and recognised something in her, there was something about her stance; it was confident but not brash. Her expression had the seriousness that the circumstances required, without coming over as stern. She had a quality that he couldn't quite place, but it was a quality he could respect. The first thing she noticed was how soft his hands were.

"Ayeka is not just Dhazi's partner," said Lutcher with a strange but slight inflection of pride in his voice. "She is not the woman behind the man, she is our equal."

Orlo said nothing, this was obvious to him as soon as their eyes met. Dhazi held the car door open, and they all got in.

One hundred metres above, a drone angled its camera down, zooming in on the four. In his penthouse, Calder watched the video feed, intrigued at the seemingly friendly interaction between these two men who had been lifelong enemies, but the presence of the other two, the man and the woman, seemed to have changed that. He was pleased, this was following a pattern foretold in several of his simulations. Since Lutcher had been spotted entering the south zone, Calder had ordered a drone to be stationed above the bridge, and as the simulations predicted, it was the next day when Orlo made the journey into the north, confirming the prediction.

The car pulled away, but Calder wasn't interested in where it was going and directed the drone to be sent somewhere else. He discouraged initiative amongst his men, no-one else had any knowledge of the simulations and could take an action that they thought would be the right thing to do but would interfere or disrupt his plans. No, he made the decisions, he made the plans, he gave the orders, and they carried them out without ever questioning them.

The video feed could have been watched by one of his men, and that person could realise that there was something going on and seek to gain favour with Calder by arresting the man and the woman. That was not part of his plan, so he selected the video records of this interaction, and of Lutcher crossing into the south zone and deleted them.

"We will go to my old headquarters, it's the last place Calder's men would expect me to go."

As they drove into the upper east side, Orlo looked out at the unfamiliar surroundings; the north was completely different to the south, all the buildings were closer together, particularly so here, and most the buildings were old and dirty.

The air seemed different too, there were hardly any trees to be seen and greenswards were churned up by vehicles having to park on them in the narrow roads. There was a dry, dusty smell mixed with exhaust gasses trapped at ground level, the high buildings all around creating dead areas, preventing wind from dispersing the fumes.

Lutcher finally saw what familiarity had prevented him seeing before: the run-down state of everything and felt slightly humbled. "The north is not like the south. The upper east side especially so."

"Once Calder is gone, we can rebuild the east zone," replied Orlo confidently.

<<<<>>>

The mood changed as the four entered the

underground room, going from serious to sombre. Ayeka noticed a change come over Lutcher, the slight anguished look that he was trying to hide.

"This is the first time I've been back, since..." He shook his head slightly. She understood the feeling he was trying to suppress and reached over, gently touching his back unseen by the other two. He momentarily closed his eyes, swallowed hard and gave a barely perceptible nod to acknowledge her comforting.

Orlo looked down at the brown stain in the concrete, then turned to Lutcher. "Is this where?..."

"Yes," he whispered, emotion finally stealing his voice.

Orlo knelt down and placed his hand on the stain. He closed his eyes and bowed his head. Without looking up, he started to speak. "I never met Sakami, but I understood what she meant to you. When I heard what happened, I felt your pain as if it were my own, and I was deeply moved when Dhazi told me of the circumstances. It was then that I first started to think of the futility of our rivalry. I am not one for prayer, prayer serves no purpose, but I am thinking of her, and of you, my friend."

Lutcher gasped as his shoulders dropped. Orlo stood up and the two old enemies embraced. "Thank you," whispered Lutcher, then he pulled away, straightened up and regained his composure. "But we have work to do."

<<<<>>>>

The four sat around a table earnestly discussing their options, with Dahzi laying out his ideas inspired by the theories in the 1027 Committee playbook.

"I have spoken to my men," said Orlo. "They understand what we are trying to achieve, they too have grown weary of the fighting. They too understand how we have been controlled."

Lutcher sat up proudly. "And I have spoken to my men. They are tired of the constant fighting, they've realised the futility. They look around and see the pointlessness of it all, but we continued, didn't we? And we would have continued. It is obvious to me now that all we were waiting for was the trigger to stop, and Dhazi is that trigger. He has given us something that has meaning, something real that we can fight for."

Orlo and Lutcher looked at each other for a moment; Ayeka could almost see the connection that was forming between the two. Both of them smiled and both dropped their shoulders slightly, both realising that the years of strife were now over.

Orlo turned to Dhazi. "We will continue to command our men, but you will be our leader. We will be generals in your army, and you command us."

Lutcher swelled with pride, his shoulders back and his head high for the first time since Sakami was killed. "What are your orders, Dhazi?"

<<<<>>>>

Four hours later the meeting broke up with an agreement for another meeting in the south zone.

That took place a few days later, with a bemused Calder watching the movements across the bridge. So far the meeting had been about the mechanics of how the two commanders – generals in the rebellion – would interact. Agreements were made and details hammered out. Emboldened by the spirit of cooperation between Lutcher and Orlo, Dhazi felt that it was time for more direct attacks, co-ordinated attacks across the north and south. The next meeting would decide what action was to be taken, and what targets would be selected.

Lutcher was leery of using his former headquarters again, so Ayeka volunteered to scout for new premises in the north.

The Safe House.

Ayeka breezed in. "I've found the perfect place for a safe house, well, it's not a house and that's the beauty of it. It's in the arcade in the old commercial district. All the shops there closed down ages ago and there's no CCTV or security to worry about."

Dhazi was impressed. "Sounds great, we're going to need it for the next meeting."

Hyodo nodded his approval. "Why don't we go there now?" his voice was flat and sombre, the way it had been since Ellie's death.

"Good idea."

<<<<>>>>

The three sauntered past the old parade.

"This one," muttered Ayeka as they passed, pointing to the barred windows and door.

"All the glass had been painted white on the inside to stop prying eyes. We'll need to go around the back to get in, the front door's locked, but the back door looks like we can force it."

Either side of the shop were burned out shells. She pointed to them. "The one on the right used to be a general store and on the left was a clothes shop. No-one's interested in this place now. Apparently, the fire brigade didn't even bother coming when these two got burned out."

The three wheeled around a corner to the rear

of the properties, making their way to the shop, stepping over the fence that had long since collapsed. The door had seen much better days, and two heaves from Dhazi's shoulder broke it open. He examined the door jamb where the wood had cracked away, noticing another lock further up that had been left unlatched.

"We'll need to replace the lock, we can't use this lower one, the striker plate's too damaged. But all we need to do is get a new lock barrel for this upper one."

"Can you fit it?" she asked.

"Sure, easy. I'll do it this afternoon."

They looked around, there was a general level of rubbish, the kind that's always left behind when a shop closes, and where the vacating occupiers have no interest in clearing up. It wasn't dirty, just a bit messy. There were two rooms on the ground floor and stairs up to another three rooms. Dhazi was satisfied that it was suitable for their needs.

<<<<>>>>

Dhazi slapped two keys down on the table, grinning. "Done."

Ayeka frowned slightly. "I'll need to go in there the day before and have a bit of a clear up, it was a bit grubby. When is the next meeting with Orlo and Lutcher?"

"A week from now."

"Do you need me to do anything?" asked Hyodo with a shake in his voice.

"Just go with Ayeka to give her a hand, but apart from that, carry on as normal. Remember, don't draw any attention."

"Okay," he mumbled, then went to his room.

Ayeka looked at him, a concerned look on her face. "He's still not okay, is he?"

"No, if anything he seems to be getting worse as time goes on. I thought he would have come to terms with it all by now."

"Loss affects everyone differently, but like you said, he may never be the same."

<<<<>>>

Hyodo paced around the flat, seemingly bothered by something. "Um, Ayeka, are you still going to safe house number two today?"

"Yeah, I want to make sure it's okay. It's been empty for a while and you know, rats can get in, besides, you saw what a mess the place was."

"Are you sure you want to go, I mean, it's probably okay in there, I doubt Lutcher would take much notice, and it's not like Orlo is staying the night." Hyodo was trying to sound nonchalant but couldn't hide the shake in his voice as he spoke to Ayeka.

"Are you alright, Hyodo?"

"No, I'm not. The more this rebellion goes on the more stressed I am getting. What if someone had told Calder where the safe houses are? Maybe we shouldn't use that one, you know, just in case."

"Only you, me, Dhazi and Lutcher know where house number two is."

"Yes, but what if Lutcher has let it slip to one of his men and they've gone on to tell someone else? It could have easily got back to Calder."

"Lutcher's solid, he won't have told anyone."

"But what if he has? I'm worried about this one and don't think you should go. Dhazi's at work, but I can get a message back to him."

"I'll be fine."

"Please don't go."

"I appreciate your concern but stop worrying."

He turned away, avoiding eye contact. "If you got caught I'd never forgive myself," he muttered.

"I'm a big girl and I can look after myself."

<<<<>>>>

They took a cautious route to the safe house to ensure nobody was following. With every step Hyodo seemed to be getting more nervous.

"You're really bothered about Lutcher, aren't you?"

"Yeah, he's a criminal."

"No, he was a criminal, but he's reformed now."

"I don't buy that. Once a criminal, always a criminal in my book. What if he's done a deal with

Calder?"

"No, that's just not possible. Calder had his wife killed, he hates the man, he would never work with him."

"Yeah, but you never really know someone, do you?" He tapped his head. "You never really know what's going on up here."

"Lighten up Hyodo, we're nearly there."

They entered the service yard to the rear of the row of disused shops. Halfway along was the building they were going to use as a safe house, Hyodo looked around anxiously.

Ayeka frowned at him. "You're drawing attention to us, that's the opposite of what you need to be doing."

"Sorry, I can't help it, I keep thinking of what Lutcher might have done."

They got to the door, Ayeka slipped the key in the lock and was just about to open it when Hyodo put his hand on her arm to stop her. "Are you sure you want to go in?"

"Yeah, the door's locked, and only Dhazi and I have keys. If Calder's men are in there then they would have had to have broken the door to get in." She looked at the door surround. "Oh look, they haven't," she muttered with amused sarcasm.

"Maybe there was another key that we didn't know about, you know, maybe the manufacturer has supplied them with a master key that can open any of these locks, or maybe they picked the lock."

She chuckled. "Dhazi put this new lock on, it's new, there are only two keys and I doubt there's a master key. Did they pick the lock? Do you really think Calder's men are that sophisticated?"

He became even more agitated. "Look, you go in, I'm going to wait outside for a bit, I wanna check the streets and make sure Calder's men aren't lurking somewhere."

"Okay."

Hyodo walked away, Ayeka watched him turn a corner and disappear from sight. She sighed and shook her head. "You worry too much," she muttered as she entered the building.

The agreed plan for all safe houses was always to enter through the back door, leaving it open for a fast escape if need be. Whoever was being met would be in the back rooms. If they weren't there, the door was to be closed to prevent anyone approaching from behind. There was no-one to meet, so she closed the door and went to a room at the front.

Suddenly the front door burst open as a sledgehammer broke the lock.

"Extermination squad," yelled a soldier, then squeezed the flame throwers' trigger, dousing the body of the female with burning fuel.

Hyodo turned a corner and was now in the street to the front of the building, he saw the flame thrower operator step back and saw the stream of fire blasting into the building; he heard the agonised shrieking from inside.

"No!" he screamed as his fears were realised in a way that in his wildest nightmare he could have never dreamed. He stood, crying and frozen by the horror, watching the soldiers get in their vehicle and leave, seemingly ambivalent to their role in this horror.

The screaming quickly faded, her suffering mercifully short, but he found himself drawn to the building, he had to see it for himself. He approached cautiously, compelled to look, but at the same time horrified as to what he would see. The door was still open, he looked in, recoiling from the heat and the thick black smoke billowing out. There on the floor was a burning body, covered in the blazing, sticky fuel, laying still, a corpse. He sank to his knees then vomited.

<<<<>>>>

He wasn't sure how long he'd been sitting there crying. The worst of the fire was out, the building was concrete and brick and there was little in there to burn. He forced himself to look back in, and retched again, the charred body had lost all of its facial features and was only vaguely recognisable as female.

"What do I tell Dhazi?" he mumbled to himself as he turned and headed back, shuffling and stumbling as he walked. All the time thinking of how to break this most terrible news, the news that his friend's girlfriend was not only dead but had died in the worst way.

He was waiting at the flat when Dhazi got home. "Where's Ayeka?" Dhazi didn't need to ask if there was a problem. Hyodo's expression, his bloodshot eyes and hunched shoulders told him that. Cold flooded through him.

"She's dead!" he cried.

Dhazi gasped and sank to his knees. Hyodo had been a joker, often making cruel jokes, but not since his parents died, he had been sombre since then, especially since the attack that saw Ellie and the others killed. He wasn't a joker anymore.

Dhazi got back up to his feet. "How? how did happen?"

"They killed her, they were waiting for us."

"How did she die?" gasped Dhazi as a wave of grief washed over him.

"Please don't make me tell you!"

The anguish in Hyodo's voice alarmed Dhazi. "How did she die?" he demanded.

Hyodo put his head in his hands and sobbed. "Fire, it was one of Calder's extermination squads."

Dhazi's vision doubled as his head swam. He remembered back to the warehouse and the rats. Hyodo staggered towards him, collapsing at his feet, howling.

"I heard her, I heard her," he gasped through sobs. "They were waiting for us. It was Lutcher, Lutcher must have told them about the safe house."

Dhazi was numbed, the full shock hadn't yet hit

him, and as the group leader he was trying to think logically. "He can't have done, I haven't told him yet." He swallowed hard at the realisation that he may have been seen changing the lock. "Someone must have seen me and reported it."

Hyodo stood up and the two men hugged each other as the full weight of the horror hit them, both crying harder than they had ever done in their lives. They stayed holding each other for a full five minutes. Finally they broke apart and slumped down into chairs. Dhazi had cried himself out, but Hyodo was inconsolable.

Dhazi stood up sharply. "I want to go and see it."

"Please don't make me go, I can't go back there," gasped Hyodo, suddenly in a state of panic at the thought of seeing Ayeka's body again.

"I'll go alone. I need to see her."

<<<<>>>>

The shop was just another blackened, burned out building that no-one would take any notice of. Dhazi approached, fearful of what he might see, Hyodo had refused to say how badly Ayeka's body had been burned, and because of that he expected the worst. He stopped outside gathering his courage, wondering if he could hold it together when he saw her.

He drew a deep breath and entered. It was worse than he feared, the face was unrecognisable, just a black featureless blob. But standing out against the charred flesh was the bright silver of the necklace he had given her. The fingers of her left hand were almost burned away, but one finger still had the ring he had bought her. He took it off.

He knelt beside her, his head bowed as he came to terms with the fact he would never see the love of his life again, the woman who drove him on, who supported him and who had made him the leader that he had become.

He tried not to think of the pain she had suffered, all that Hyodo had said was that it didn't last long. It was a tiny bit of comfort in what was the worst day of his life. He took the ring and the necklace in case someone found the body and stole them, he couldn't bear the thought of someone else wearing them.

He didn't feel angry, his sorrow was blocking that emotion – at the moment, though he knew that when it emerged, he would have a rage like no other and would have to fight hard to keep it in check.

He stood up, it was time to let Ayeka's parents know.

<<<<>>>>

He spared them the details, the mother was distraught enough as it was. Her father sat staring at a wall, unblinking in his grief.

"She always said that she wouldn't make old bones, and that she would go before us," he muttered. "I thought we'd have a few more years, though."

"It was Calder's men."

He sighed deeply. "I don't have the strength for the fight anymore. You will have to fight for me."

"I will avenge her death. But we can't leave her there."

The father's shoulders dropped. "Come on, let's get it over with."

<<<<>>>>

There was silence in the car as they drove to the site. The father in shock, trying to come to terms with everything, and Dhazi trying not to think about the enormous hole in his life now that she was gone.

Eventually the father spoke, he didn't look at Dhazi, instead he stared straight ahead as if talking to someone else. "There's talk of a resistance movement, quiet talk. We've all seen the graffiti, and we all know about the attacks on the police cars. Those kids that were killed? That was harsh even by Calder's standards, so there has to be something going on, Ayeka would have wanted to be part of that."

"She was…"

He put his hand up to silence Dhazi. "Don't tell me, it's best if I don't know." There was a long period of silence as he weighed up how much to tell the young man. "She knew something of my past, but I hadn't told her everything. I was a commander in the 1027 Committee. A compatriot of mine was captured and made to talk, and I don't need to tell you how that was done. He gave them some names, but he didn't give me up, even though he could have saved himself if he did. A lot of people were executed, it finished us.

"She had spirit. I always knew she would take up the fight one day. She knew the risks, I had told her how dangerous it would be, but it made no difference, you know how single minded she could be."

Dhazi sighed and hung his head. There was another long period of silence.

"Tell me how she died."

"Please, Mr Beka, I can't…"

"Tell me!" he demanded.

Dhazi told Ayeka's father exactly what had happened. The father listened in silence, his face slowly melting from horror into anguish, all the time fighting back tears. "I won't ever tell her mother what happened."

<<<<>>>

Neither man could face touching the charred corpse, but both knew they had to. The father had brought an old carpet and together, and with both stoic they rolled the body up in it. The only saving grace being that the rats hadn't found her. They carried her to the car with all the dignity they could muster, placing her on the back seat.

Dhazi wiped his eyes and calmed himself. "What do we do with her? She can't have a regular funeral."

"I know someone, he works at the crem'. He was from 1027 back in the day, he got disillusioned with the lack of progress and left. I didn't know him that well, I just hope he recognises me."

<<<<>>>>

The man didn't recognise him, but five hundred credits ensured that he asked no questions. He pointed to an empty coffin.

"Put it in there, I'll do it first thing tomorrow when I'm warming up the oven. Nobody's counting nowadays."

His demeanour and his referring to the body as 'it' made it obvious that he had disposed of bodies like this before. It seemed callous, and it bothered Ayeka's father, but Dhazi realised that it was just an ambivalent attitude borne of thirty years of working there, burning bodies and becoming immune to the wails of the weeping relatives.

Dhazi saw that the man who would have been his father-in-law was only just holding it together. He turned to the technician. "Can you give us a bit of time."

"Whatever. I'm going out for a smoke, will that be enough?"

"Yes, thank you."

They fixed the lid on the coffin Ayeka's father finally broke down, and for a second time Dhazi had to suppress his own massive sense of loss to comfort another.

"How will you explain her disappearance?"

"I'll say she's gone off somewhere to live on her own. You saw how independent she…" he choked on his words as he remembered his daughter. "...how independent she was. Nobody will be surprised."

Dhazi swallowed hard, he felt he had to apologise to the man but couldn't think of the words. "Mr Beka I am so, so very sorry. If we hadn't met you'd..."

He put his hand up to silence Dhazi. "Because of me, her life was chaotic, always wondering when the next six-in-the-morning raid would be. With you she'd found a purpose, a fight she felt she could win. She was happy. Remember her for that."

Orlo And Lutcher.

Dhazi dragged himself out of bed, his pillow was cold and wet where he'd cried himself to sleep. He looked over to her side of the bed. Now it was empty. All her things were still on the bedside table. Her trinkets remained where she had left them. Nothing in life now would be the same, yet nothing had changed. Except she was gone. He could smell her presence, the light perfume that she wore still hung in the air, eventually it would vanish.

It was torture for him to see all her items, but he couldn't bring himself to get rid of them, he would leave them exactly as they were. He went to his jacket and took out the necklace and ring, placing them with all her other possessions.

By now she'd have been up, dressed and making him breakfast, he'd have a shower then go down and they'd chat about what they wanted to do. He went to the bathroom and was shocked at his haggard reflection in the mirror.

"I can't be like this, it'll be an insult to her memory."

As he stood under the shower, his immense sadness slowly morphed into anger, and he stepped out of the shower a different man to when he got in. As he left the bathroom he came face to face with Hyodo, who instantly broke down crying. Dhazi knew he had to be strong for his friend, and as the leader he had to be strong for everyone, but it would be hard without her by his side.

"It's not your fault, Hyodo."

Hyodo looked up at him, a pitiful expression of utter anguish on his face. "I loved her," he gasped then broke down crying again. Dhazi picked him up and led him to a couch.

Although he didn't want to, Dhazi realised that they both needed to eat, and struggled with his emotions as he looked through the cupboards that she had kept so well stocked. He tried to focus his mind, but his thoughts kept coming back to her last moments and the unspeakable pain she must have suffered.

"How could they have done that to her?" he muttered as he thought of the soldier pointing his weapon at her. His confused feelings of rage, sadness, hatred and loss finally got the better of him and he pounded the worktop with his fists. Then, as abruptly as it had started, he stopped, pulled himself up straight. He turned to Hyodo.

"We need to inform Lutcher and Orlo."

Hyodo looked up at him, terrified. "I can't, I can't face them."

"Okay, I'll go on my own."

<<<<>>>

Dhazi just about retained his dignity as he told the two men what had happened. In a way, he was glad Hyodo wasn't there, his friend's devastation at witnessing Ayeka's death was total. If Hyodo broke down in front of Lutcher and Orlo, then he would too, and he needed to be strong if he was ever to avenge her death.

As he laid out the events, Lutcher's expression slowly changed from disbelief, to shock, through sadness, then finally to anger. He started to pace around, snorting like a bull, clenching his fists. Anger got the better of him and he punched the side of a cupboard, cracking the wood. He ignored the blood dripping from his knuckles and turned to Dhazi.

"I loved her too, not the way you did, but I loved her for the person she was. I would have done anything to protect her."

"I know you would, and I thank you for it."

Throughout the time Dhazi had been talking, Orlo's expression had remained calm but with an undercurrent of menace. He put his hand on Dhazi's shoulder. "Calder will pay dearly for this. But we must make our plans, we must not rush in."

Lutcher stood beside Orlo, his one-time enemy but now his friend. "At this moment all I want to do is to snap the neck of anyone associated with Calder. But Orlo is right, we have to plan this, and you need to learn how to fight."

Orlo looked Dhazi up and down. "You have mental strength, but like me, you do not have physical strength. So I will teach you to fight the way I learned to, you will fight with your head, I will show you how to anticipate an opponent's move, how to dodge a blow and how to respond. I will show you how to feign defeat to lull your opponent into a false sense of security, so they will drop their guard. And most importantly, how to channel your rage and not let it cloud your judgement, because the fight will be hard."

Lutcher nodded approvingly. "And I will teach you brawn; you will fight with your heart. I will show you how to use your strength efficiently, where on the body to strike for maximum effect, how to conserve energy and how to remove all pity from your mind. You are a compassionate person, and pity will be your greatest enemy."

Both men had just described to Dhazi the way their men had fought each other, often killing each other, but now both men had set aside their history for the greater good of all Matrea.

Hyodo's Arrest.

Two days after it happened, Lutcher, Orlo and Hyodo got together in Dhazi's flat and sat around the table discussing a suitable date for an attack on the palace. Dhazi had told them what he wanted to do, and Lutcher and Orlo had started to work together to refine the plan that Dhazi had memorised from the book Ayeka's father had given her. Hyodo had been inconsolable and only briefly took part. Dhazi had set aside his grief, he was the group leader and had to be strong, anything less would be an insult to her memory. Without her he would have not become the man he was now.

The date had been decided, two months from now her death would be avenged. Then he would allow himself to grieve.

<<<<>>>>

Dhazi sat staring at the wall. Three days had now passed, and the immediate horror of Ayeka's death had worn off but had been replaced with a brooding hatred deeper than he ever thought he was capable of. Orlo had urged him to be calm, to not rush into things, but to make careful plans. Both Lutcher and Orlo had pledged their men in support of the action he had chosen to take.

He was absentmindedly running her necklace through his fingers. He had wanted to keep it, even though he knew he would never give it to anyone else; he would never feel the same way about anyone ever again.

When he took it off her body, he had wanted to keep it to know that part of her DNA was near him, but the smell of the fuel was still there, it was faint, but it was too much of a reminder. He turned on a tap and held the ring under the flow for a few minutes, then dried it with a cloth.

It was clean now, and he actually preferred it. Water may have washed away the last trace of her, but it sparkled the way she did, it brought a brightness to the room the way she had done. The ring was the same, it was just as shiny. It had been a good fit on her slender ring finger but would only just fit the tip of his little finger, and he found himself constantly trying to slip it all the way over.

He was unaware that Hyodo wasn't at the flat until he came in late in the evening. While Dhazi was calm but sombre, Hyodo was agitated and skittish, seemingly more affected by the event than Dhazi. He put this down to Hyodo having witnessed the incident, but he didn't know just how deeply his friend had been affected.

"Where have you been?"

"I went for a long walk, I had to try and get my head straight."

"And did you?"

"I got some things sorted out. I now know what I'm going to do." There was an undercurrent of positivity to Hyodo's voice, a tone that had been missing since his parents died. It was subtle, but it was there.

"What are you going to do?"

"I'm not going to say. All I will say is that you don't need me anymore, you'll be stronger without me."

"Hyodo, what do you mean?"

"You have been good to me all these years, you looked after me. Ayeka looked after me. I loved her like a big sister, but now she's gone, and I have to go too."

"Don't do anything stupid. What happened to Ayeka was not your fault, whatever it is that you're planning to do, think very carefully about it. You may not realise it, but I need you."

"No you don't, I'll let you down, I'll always let you down. Anyway, I'm tired and I'm going to bed."

"Well if you're not going to tell me what it is, then the least you can do is tell me when."

"You'll know."

<<<<>>>>

Hyodo crept out of bed at three in the morning, tiptoeing through the flat so as to not wake Dhazi. Satisfied that he hadn't, he opened the door as quietly as possible and left, taking the spare lock-up key with him. Walking in the shadows, he made his way to the garage, entering through the side door taking the blackout curtain that Ayeka had made and pulling it across the door so he could turn the light on.

On the floor was a can of petrol, some oil, and some

plastic foam. There were also glass bottles, a bucket and rags. He remembered something his father had told him over and over again.

'*To be a man you must repay every debt.*' Ayeka's death was a loss, in his mind it was a debt. He would be repaying this debt in kind.

He also remembered the formula, the one that she had come up with, and set about mixing the various ingredients in a bucket until the correct viscosity was reached. Enough petrol to make the mixture flow, enough oil to keep it burning and enough plastic dissolved in the solution to make it stick.

He carefully decanted the liquid into a glass bottle, stuffing a rag in the top. It was four thirty. He would avenge her death at six, when the first patrol of the day passed through. There would be enough people on the streets heading to work to witness him repaying the debt.

"Two lives for a life," he muttered as he sat down to centre his thoughts and make peace with himself. He didn't now care for his own life. Though he was bothered that he could implicate Dhazi, but realised the garage was far enough away from the flat to not incriminate him. He'd left the lock-up key in the garage and had not taken his key to the flat. There was no way an investigation could tie Dhazi to him or the action he was going to take, and when he was interrogated he would insist he had acted alone, regardless of how they tried to force information from him.

At five thirty he stood up, checked that his lighter

worked, picked up the bottle and went outside just as the sun broke over the horizon. He walked to the street corner where he knew the car would soon pass.

"I'm doing this for you, Ayeka," he whispered to himself.

There were a few people about, all making their way to work. Some were grumbling about it, others accepting of the routine and none of them taking any notice of him, but in about five minutes that would change.

He heard it, the low revving throb of a powerful engine pulling the car through the streets. The side windows would be open, because the windows were always open, it made it easier for Calder's men to shout abuse or yell at people just because they could. They would pass within three metres of him; he got ready, practicing in his mind what he would do. Timing would be critical, he couldn't light the rag too soon or it might be spotted, too late and he might miss.

There were no other cars on the road, people usually walked to the tube or bus station, most heading to the central northern zone. He glanced around and saw that there were a few people heading towards him on his side of the road. Hearing the approaching car and seeing their distance he was able to quickly calculate that they would be far enough away when he stepped into the road and threw the petrol bomb into the car, the bottle shattering on the dashboard and dousing the occupants with burning fuel.

He would not run, he would stand and watch, he

wanted to hear their pitiful screams, like the ones he had heard from her. He wanted to watch them trying to wipe away the blazing gel only to spread it further as the fuel sticks to their hands, as it must have done to hers. He wanted to see them get out flailing their arms as they fall to the ground, writhing in agony the way she would have done. When he was satisfied that they were at the point of no return, he would slowly walk away with his head held high.

He had no plan for what to do next but didn't care. Ayeka's death would have been avenged, and people would see that they could make a stand and hit back at Calder. Maybe it would strike a bit of fear into Calder's men, maybe they might start to feel vulnerable and not be so quick with their harassment of the people.

The car was close. He tensed; a bead of sweat formed on his brow and was about to run into his eye, he wiped it away with his sleeve. He picked up the bottle, then took out his lighter, flicking on the flame and touching it to the rag. His timing was perfect, the blue flame turning into bright yellow just as the car drew level. He stepped forward.

"Death to Calder, long live the 1027 Committee," he yelled as he hurled the petrol bomb at the open window. But the window was shut, the bottle shattered against the bulletproof glass, spraying fuel all over the side of the car. Nothing happened for a fraction of a second, then the burning rag ignited the fuel and the car erupted in flames, though only one side was on fire.

He saw the door on the other side open and an officer start to get out. Suddenly gripped with fear he turned and ran, expecting people to get out of his way. He also expected that all the people were against Calder and sick of the repression by his men. The thought that Calder had supporters within the population didn't enter his head. So he wasn't prepared for the fist to his face that knocked him out.

<<<<>>>>

Dhazi woke to the sound of sirens and the blue flashing lights of squad cars thundering down the streets. He looked out of the window and saw multiple vehicles converging on an area where a column of thick black smoke was rising up. He glanced around into Hyodo's room and saw the bed was empty.

"Hyodo, what have you done?" he gasped.

He pulled on some clothes and left the flat, mingling in with the rest of the curious making their way to the scene. Behind them, the blaring horn of a fire engine forced everyone off the road. As he got close to the lock-up, he ducked out of the flow of people and went to its side door. No-one took any notice of him, all were focussed on the bright yellow and orange flames that were now lighting up the surrounding buildings.

Once inside, Dhazi saw the missing bottle and smelled the fuel mixture; confirming he what realised Hyodo had done but had no idea of what the target had been. He assumed that his friend would lie low for a while before returning to the flat; he didn't know Hyodo had been caught.

He left the lock-up and mingled back in with the crowd. Soon the still blazing car came into view, with fire crews making ready to put it out. He gasped as he realised the enormity of his friend's actions, and the repercussion following the attempt to kill two police officers. Now he knew why Hyodo had been a little bit more focussed; he had tried to avenge Ayeka, but it looked like he had failed.

"Do we know what happened here?" he nonchalantly asked no-one in particular.

"I heard it was a petrol bomb," came a reply from a man old enough to be his father.

"Do they know who did it?"

"I don't know, I've only just got here myself, but maybe it was the same guy that did the power hub, no-one believes it was lightning." The man paused and thought for a bit, then lowered his voice. "It obviously wasn't a lightning strike on the security building either, so he must have had an accomplice, he couldn't have done both himself." The man paused. "Shame it didn't burn the place down," he muttered quietly.

'Great' Dhazi thought to himself, 'the message is getting through.'

"'bout time someone stood up to them bastards," the man muttered as he walked away.

Angry looking police, hyped up by the attack on their colleagues, moved towards the crowd, riot batons drawn and raised above their head, ready to strike anyone who didn't immediately obey their commands. The crowd didn't wait to be told and swiftly dispersed. Dhazi left with them, he's seen what he needed to see, and heard what he wanted to hear.

He turned on his TV to see what coverage there would be on the news and what lies they would cast. It opened with a view of a courtroom. He stepped through all of the channels, all had the same video feed. This was only done where there was a charge of treason.

"Oh no!" he sighed as he realised the significance. His shoulders dropped. "They've got Hyodo."

<<<<>>>>

In the eleven years since the execution of the teacher, and the subsequent crushing of the resurgent 1027 Committee, there had been no further trials for treason. No other trials were ever televised, as no-one wanted to see the one-sided proceedings; the charade that passed for justice. Concern for others was considered a weakness in Matrea, so being a defence lawyer was seen as an undesirable career. Defence was the occupation for newly qualified, inexperienced lawyers. In time they all moved into prosecution because the prestige and kudos was in prosecution, where arrogance and brutal questioning would browbeat the defence counsel and corner the defendant. Testimonies were twisted, forcing the accused into submission and confess their guilt in court, even if they had committed no crime.

Upon being made aware of the arrest of Hyodo, Calder had issued two new decrees: from now on there would be no lawyers in a treason trial, guilt or innocence would be decided by a tribunal of the three most senior judges in Matrea.

They would examine evidence and call witnesses, then decide the fate of the accused. The outcome would be a forgone conclusion, and a guilty verdict had only one sentence, death. The second decree was that the sentence, when carried out, would also be broadcast live.

All television channels would cease regular programming to show the event, and this would serve as a warning to those watching of the dangers of treachery. It would send a particularly strong message to the nascent band of dissidents that had attacked the power supply to the combined security building and whom Calder knew had been encouraging the spread of graffiti.

Hyodo sat in a prison cell, his nose broken and dried blood on his face; no attempt had been made to treat his injuries or clean him up. The pounding in his head had only just stopped when the door burst open, and two guards entered. They said nothing as they hauled him to his feet and dragged him up the stairs and into the courtroom.

Back at the flat, Dhazi sank down into a chair as he saw the image of his friend emerge and noticed the blood on his face and the blackening around his eyes.

Hyodo stood in the dock, his heart thumping in his chest. He looked all around and saw scowling faces staring at him. A cameraman was fiddling with his equipment, adjusting zoom and focus for the best shot; this was a treason trial and he had to get it right.

Every image had to be perfect and every sound clearly audible, his future career depended on it.

Hyodo swayed on his feet, partly from the injury to his head and partly through the overwhelming situation. He reached to the side of the dock for support but got a rap over the knuckles from a cane.

"Keep your eyes to the front and your hands by your side, traitor!" snarled a voice in his ear.

"All rise," yelled a court orderly.

Three stern judges appeared, each one glowering at Hyodo as they took their places. They conferred for a couple of minutes, tapping on computer keyboards and shuffling papers. Then the head judge turned to the court clerk. "Read out the charges."

The clerk stood, nodded respectfully to the judges then turned to Hyodo.

"This court charges the defendant, Hyodo Simu, with treason in the first degree, in that, charge 1: The defendant called for the death of our leader. Charge 2: The defendant attempted to murder two police officers. Charge 3: The defendant was in possession of, an offensive weapon. Charge 4: The defendant destroyed police property. Charge 5: The defendant attempted to flee the scene. Charge 6: The defendant shouted the name of a proscribed organisation. All of these are contrary to the law."

The clerk sat down and the judges conferred again, making notes and seeming to take far longer than was necessary. Dhazi realised what this was: it was theatre, a show to give the impression that the outcome hadn't already been decided. Eventually they stopped and the lead judge addressed Hyodo.

"How do you plead, traitor?" His voice had none of the snarling aggression that Dhazi expected; it was soft, measured, but that didn't hide the undertone of menace.

Hyodo sighed and his shoulders dropped a fraction, then he pulled himself up straight, a look of defiance on his face. He looked the judge in the eye. "Guilty! Guilty of all of them."

He turned and looked directly into the camera lens. "And I'm proud of it," he shouted. Everyone in the courtroom gasped.

The judges scowled at him. "Guilty, what!?" one of them demanded.

Hyodo leant forward, grabbing the dock leaning out sneering at the judges and baring his teeth. He ignored the rap from the cane across his knuckles. "I am not going to say, 'Your Honour' because that would mean I respect this court, and I don't." He pointed at everyone in the room. "Not one of you have honour that I can respect, you're all Calder's puppets."

A second and third crack of the cane saw him release his grip and stand back. He ignored the pain in his hands, he could have rubbed them to ease it but was determined to show no weakness.

A hubbub rose from the people in the courtroom. The lead judge banged his gavel.

"Silence in court," yelled the clerk.

The judge pointed at Hyodo. "This court accepts your guilt, and it is now the job of the court to examine the events. Bring in the first witness."

One by one people were brought in to testify. The first were Calder's men from the car. Large images of the burned out vehicle appeared on screens. There were people from the street who had witnessed everything, and it appeared to Dhazi that some may have been coerced into giving evidence. The last witness was the man who had taken Hyodo down.

"…and what is it that you heard the defendant say," asked the lead judge.

The man stared hard at Hyodo. "Your Honour, I clearly heard the traitor say, 'Death to Calder, long live the 1027 Committee'."

A shocked gasp rose from all assembled and people started to mutter to each other. The lead judge had to bang his gavel three times to silence them.

"That in itself is treason," he growled ominously. The judges conferred, and again took longer than was necessary, all three eventually nodding in agreement; the lead judge glowered at Hyodo. "Taking to account all the charges, in particular your call for our leader's death as laid out in charge number one, it is the unanimous decision of this court that the only appropriate punishment is death by hanging. And as this is for treason, no appeal is allowed; the sentence is to be carried out immediately."

Dhazi felt sick as he saw the judge and heard the words, then the camera turned to Hyodo. He was not crestfallen but held his head high. Conflicting emotions surged through Dhazi, a desperate sadness fighting against an immense pride at his friend's courage.

The clerk of the court opened the sentencing book and read the legally required text.

"Hyodo Simu, you have pleaded guilty to treason, which is punishable by death. You will now be taken from this place to a place of execution where you will be hanged by the neck until you are dead."

"Take him away," snapped the judge.

Rough hands grabbed Hyodo, he didn't resist but shouted "Death to Calder" as he was taken away.

The camera feed switched to a courtyard, in the centre was the gallows scaffold. Though horrified, Dhazi would not turn off the TV, but instead would watch the execution in the faint hope that Hyodo would know that he was watching and that it might give him some grains of comfort in his last moments. Ten silent minutes passed, then he saw his friend being led to the steps, his hands tied behind his back, the bag already over his head. Guards guided him up and onto the platform, then tied his feet together. The executioner placed the noose around his neck and tightened the knot, muttering something as he eased Hyodo's head to one side.

Hyodo didn't tremble, there was no flapping of

the hood where he was desperately gasping his last breaths. He would show no ignominy, instead he stood stoically in acceptance of his fate. No words were spoken to him, no repetition of the sentence, no last rites.

The guards stepped back, the executioner pulled the lever, trap doors opened beneath Hyodo's feet and he disappeared from view. Half a second later the rope snapped tight, and Hyodo's life was over.

Though immensely sad, Dhazi couldn't cry; in the space of a week, he had lost Ayeka, the love of his life, murdered in the most horrific way on the orders of Calder. And now he had just witnessed the death of his best friend because of Calder. Instead of tears, his sadness was channelled into a rage, but for the time being he still had to suppress that rage.

The broadcast switched to the news for an instant analysis of the trial and execution. A sombre looking presenter looked up from his computer screen and frowned into the camera lens.

'*Well there we have it, a trial for treason, and the justifiable execution of the traitor Hyodo Simu. It is the first treason trial in many years and let's hope this execution will serve as a deterrent to anyone else foolish enough to challenge* authority. *The police say that Hyodo Simu was mentally disturbed by the death of his parents and had no accomplices. The police say he acted alone and are not looking for anyone else in connection with this heinous event. With me to discuss mental illness is...*'

Dhazi turned the TV off, disgusted but not

surprised. "Hyodo was distraught, but he was not mentally ill," he grumbled to himself.

Lutcher and Orlo, his two commanders of divisions in the growing army, had been discussing a plan, it was time to refine it for the date that they had chosen.

<<<<>>>>

Over the next few weeks, every free moment was spent in training. With Lutcher building up Dhazi's strength, engaging in physical combat with him. Lutcher encouraged Dhazi to hit him as hard as he could but had restricted his own blows to light slaps to Dhazi's head and face, taunting Dhazi to punch him on the nose, building his speed and aggression and nurturing the brooding hatred.

"How did you feel when you saw Hyodo in court?" chuckled Lutcher as he blocked a punch, then tapped Dhazi's cheek.

"Shocked."

"Good." Lutcher blocked another punch, then slapped, and went to quickly slap again, though Dhazi was able to block the second strike. Lutcher smiled, the training was working, but he was able to hit Dhazi across the top of his head with another slap that he didn't see coming.

"So how did you feel when you saw him on the gallows with a noose around his neck, his head cocked to one side to make his neck snap?"

"I was proud of him."

"And how did you feel when you saw him drop, and the rope tighten as his neck snapped?"

Dhazi stood snorting with anger, but said nothing.

"What will you do when you meet Calder?"

"Kill him," he hissed through clenched teeth.

"What will you do to Calder's men?" Dhazi ducked away from a slap that just missed his cheek.

"KILL THEM ALL!" he shouted as he charged at Lutcher, absorbing a couple of slaps while throwing a flurry of punches, forcing Lutcher back as he fended them off. Eventually, a punch from Dhazi made contact with Lutcher's chin, he staggered back and Dhazi went for him again, a second punch landing square on the nose. Lutcher put his hands up defensively, it was the first time he'd done that.

"Good hit," he muttered as he wiped blood from his top lip. He looked at Dhazi and saw the aggression still in his eyes. "I think you're nearly ready."

Orlo's training was more subtle, focussing on speed and agility, recognising threats and avoiding them. They used sticks instead of knives, with Orlo pointing out the areas of the body that were not protected by armour, but that could be struck to incapacitate an opponent before a final fatal strike.

<<<<>>>>

The time was drawing near, the training was almost over and it was time to prepare and give Dhazi final pieces of advice.

"The praetorian guards have body armour, but it is incomplete. Remember what I have shown you. I will give you a knife. You will kill a guard with it then take his weapon and fight your way into the palace." Orlo produced a knife and handed it to Dhazi. He drew it from its sheath. The blade was about fifteen centimetres long tapering from a needle-sharp point to thirty millimetres wide at its midpoint before narrowing down to the hilt, forming a shallow, rounded diamond shape.

"I've never seen a knife like this before."

"It is a thrusting weapon, the shape allows for ease of penetration. I have personally sharpened it for you."

Dhazi felt the edge, it was razor sharp. Orlo looked at the weapon, the faintest hint of a smile breaking on his usually inscrutable face. "It was my first, and it seems appropriate for you to have it."

"Thank you."

"Don't take the assault rifle, they're heavy and will slow you down," warned Lutcher. "Take the side arm and enough magazines that you have time to collect. Hold the weapon with both hands and with your arms slightly bent. There will be a switch on the side, it's the safety, make sure it's off. You've seen action films, so you know the sort of thing you have to do."

Lutcher's face grew solemn as he drew two fingers across his eyes and then down either side of his nose, forming a broad 'T'. "A shot anywhere here will be an instant kill. But the head is a small target and moves too much, you will need to get close to guarantee a hit, too close. The gun is powerful, but its bullets won't penetrate the chest armour, though the force of a shot will knock them over. Then it's a shot to the groin, where there is a gap between the thigh armour and the lower body protection. This will sever the femoral artery; they will bleed to death, but it will be messy, and they won't die straight away. The praetorian guards are tough, and even though they know they won't survive for more than a couple of minutes, they will still be able to fire their weapons at you."

Orlo could see the concern on Dhazi's face. "You must remember that the palace guards are fanatics, their devotion to Calder is absolute, and they will fight to the very last moment of their lives to defend him. To succeed in your mission, you will need to kill them, you will have no choice."

Luther nodded in agreement. "Orlo is right. A shot to the groin will kill them, but to end them quickly, aim for the face."

Dhazi's face darkened, a look of determination in his eyes. "Ayeka didn't die quickly, so neither will they."

<<<<>>>>

Dhazi hid his contempt for the police as he handed out the drinks, as ever, playing the humble waiter as he took their food orders. Though he noticed a change in their demeanour, the arrogance had gone, replaced with a look of concern. He had long since trained himself to hide his feelings when dealing with these odious men but smiled inside as he looked at the glum expressions on their faces.

The men ate and drank in relative silence, a far cry from their usual vulgar attitude. Normally they would talk loudly about whatever harassment they had delivered that day. But now their conversation was muted, especially from the man who had challenged Dhazi's father all those years ago, who seemed to be some sort of self-appointed leader.

Something was up and was bothering the men. The microphone was still in place and Dhazi desperately needed them to talk about their fears.

They finished their meal and left early to the relief of the other patrons who visibly relaxed and stayed longer as a result. Dhazi was relieved but concerned that as they had been talking quietly, the microphone might not have picked up anything that they had said. The restaurant was normally empty by ten thirty, but tonight, because of the lack of the police, it was nearly midnight before he could retrieve the USB stick.

He wasted no time in loading the file onto his computer, and to his relief, what they had said was clearly audible, and their words, telling.

<<<<>>>>

The three men sat around the table in Dhazi's flat. Since losing Ayeka it had become untidy, he hadn't realised how much tidying up of his mess that she had done. He couldn't bring himself to clear up, as a tidy flat would be too much of a reminder for him.

A calendar was open with a date they had decided

on.

"Calder is getting complacent," announced Dhazi as he got his computer, loaded the file from the previous night and clicked, 'Play'. "Listen to this," he said as he scrolled to a significant section of the recording.

"...and all the Praetorian guards have been removed from the palace. There's a whole new bunch of guards, they're hopeless," came the voice of one of the police officers above the sounds of the restaurant. "Not even second grade," he grumbled.

"What's wrong with them?" came another voice.

"They're just incompetent. I had to go there, the ones that I saw were overweight slobs just lounging around. Calder's reduced the numbers and some of the checkpoints weren't even manned. The barracks were empty! There can't be more than fifty guards in the whole place. It took half an hour just to get my permit stamped. And I tell you this, the ones that are there are not like the old guards, I don't mind admitting that I used to be a bit afraid of them."

"Perhaps Calder doesn't need top of the line guards anymore."

"Yeah, because we do all the work now, don't we?" came a third, slightly bitter voice. "How long is it going to be before one of us gets a petrol bomb in the face?"

"They're rattled," smirked Lutcher.

Orlo reached over and stopped the playback. "How do we know what he's saying is genuine?. It could be a trap."

"I don't think so," said Dhazi, confidently. "There was something about their manner, they weren't cocky like they usually are. They actually seemed a bit depressed and it's the first time I've heard anything even close to a criticism of Calder."

Lutcher scoffed. "Yeah, because now they know what it's like to be on the receiving end."

Dhazi thought for a moment. "Yes, that's why they've been coming down hard with the stop and search, that's going to work in our favour. We reduced the amount of graffiti directed at Calder, so maybe he feels safer now that the police are doing all the work."

Orlo pondered the date they had selected. "The 1027 Committee always chose dates that were significant to Calder."

"We chose this date to be as far away from any anniversary, so perhaps he feels safe at the moment. And if what this man has said is true, then our numbers will easily match theirs. This is the time to strike."

Attack On The Palace.

The forces gathered at their assigned positions, fifty of Lutcher's men to attack from the north and fifty of Orlo's men to attack from the south. The leaders were all together at the riverside in the northern industrial zone. Dhazi would use the same tactic that the teacher had used, floating downstream in a barrel, though this time he would have the distraction of the attack on the palace to draw guards away.

Dhazi raised his head proudly. "From the rumours I have heard, I believe that once they see the attack on the palace, the people will come out and join us. We will show them that there is nothing to fear if we all stand together." Then he seemed to shrink down a fraction. "If only Ayeka was here to see it."

Lutcher embraced Dhazi holding him tight. "Remember Ayeka and channel your rage, just as I will remember Sakami and channel mine," he whispered as anger stole his voice.

Orlo bowed his head. "I have never suffered such depths of grief as you two, but I feel your pain, I feel your sorrow. I will remember them, and it will be an honour to fight this fight and avenge their deaths.

The three men synchronised their watches then shook hands. Dhazi looked at them, an immense feeling of pride filling him. "Today, in an hours' time, we change Matrea and reset the clock. Some of us may not make it, but it's what we have to do. I do this for Matrea, and I do this for Ayeka." A faint smile broke on his face. "I'll see you on the other side."

He lowered himself into the barrel. Lutcher pushed it out into the river's flow, then the two men rejoined their respective gangs.

As with the teacher, the first bridge was easy, as was the second, the guards too busy scanning the roads to notice rubbish in the river. There was less detritus but still enough for the barrel to pass anonymously. Since settling on this plan, Dhazi had studied the river, and in particular, the fork that would take him towards the palace. He noticed that one side was more turbulent, and he would need to steer towards the opposite bank.

In the gap between bridge one and two, he managed to manoeuvre into the correct position, and though his progress slowed, he should be able to stay in the calmer waters.

<<<<>>>

Lutcher's van was gathering speed as it hurtled towards the palace. Behind him were six other vans full of his men.

"No sentries," he muttered, slightly puzzled, as they approached the gate.

To the south, Orlo's men were getting ready to scale the wall.

To the rear of the palace, Dhazi approached the jetty. Using his hands, he silently brought the barrel to a stop, grabbing hold of an upright, and pulling himself under the boardwalk to stay out of sight. He checked his watch. "Any minute now," he muttered as he pulled himself up out of the barrel and onto the steps leading up. He took a chance and peered over the edge to see a lone guard by the entrance. A quick glance around showed him the route he could take, a wall, about ten metres long was partially in shadow and led right to the entrance.

Lutcher's van crashed through the gates, smashing them off their hinges as the convoy careened towards the palace. Guards emerged and started firing wildly as they lumbered forward. Lutcher gave the signal and the convoy separated and his men spilled out, taking up positions behind the statues, returning fire, safe in the knowledge that the guards would be reluctant to hit the granite effigies.

At the rear of the palace, Dhazi heard the distant gunfire and saw the guard turn around, exactly as he expected. He took advantage of the distraction to climb up onto the jetty and move swiftly to the relative shadow on the wall. The guard seemed fixated on the sounds of the battle and stayed with his back turned, failing to hear Dhazi's silent approach, and oblivious to the danger.

Dhazi drew his knife as he got close, then paused. He thought of Ayeka, the beautiful woman he had loved so intensely. He thought of her personality and all the things she had done for him. Then his mind darkened as he thought of the agony she had suffered in her last moments. Then the image of what was left of her burned face filled his mind, and a righteous anger exploded inside him.

He ran to the man, who finally heard something

and turned, but too late. Dhazi thrust the knife up and into the man's throat between the helmet's chin strap and the high collar of his armoured tunic. The unprotected area gave no resistance to the blade as it penetrated the larynx and on to the spine, separating the vertebrae and severing the spinal cord. Dhazi felt no pity as the man slumped dead to the ground. He took the guard's pistol and spare magazines, flicked off the safety, then made his way in. Ahead there was a commotion as more guards made their way to the front of the palace.

Outside and to the south, Orlo's men were pouring over the wall to out-flank the guards, who seemed to be confused and leaderless.

Some of the guards moved forward in futile attempts to gain ground, only to be cut down. Orlo's men didn't have guns, they didn't need them, they would use their knives and stealth. The moment had arrived. Orlo pressed a key on his phone, sending a signal to Lutcher.

"Cease fire," Lutcher shouted to his men. The guards also stopped firing and stared ahead, confused... until Orlo's men charged through their ranks, cutting them down. Lutcher waved his men on as they charged into the melee.

<<<<>>>

Dhazi crept slowly forward, making his way upstairs, heading toward the penthouse where he knew Calder would be. He saw a guard station, it was unmanned, and he could see that the CCTV monitors were all blank. He crept past and turned a corner to find a guard with his back turned; the guard wasn't wearing the armoured tunic, just a shirt. Dhazi wasted no time in grabbing the man and driving his knife into the man's back. Another guard suddenly appeared, also not in the standard uniform, the man raised his weapon but was slow and seemed confused. Dhazi raised his weapon and pulled the trigger, but nothing happened, the gun was empty. Puzzled, Dhazi discarded the weapon and leapt forward tackling the man to the ground. A few hard blows to the man's face rendered him senseless and unable to resist as a knife was pushed into his heart.

Dhazi sheathed the knife took the man's gun and checked that this one had a loaded magazine. Holding the gun, he ran along a corridor pushing at doors until one swung open. He dived inside ready to shoot anyone he saw.

Adrenaline surged through him, giving him the strength to sprint up the stairs in front of him, taking three steps at a time. He emerged into a corridor and saw three guards ahead, they turned and started to raise their weapons, but their movements were also slow, and they too were not wearing any body armour. He was deep in the palace and these were not the praetorian guards. Dhazi felt emboldened, the intel was right. Three shots killed all three men.

<<<<>>>>

Outside, the slaughter continued, Lutcher and Orlo had lost men, but many more guards had been killed in the hand to hand fighting. Suddenly, Lutcher heard a voice above the cacophony of battle, a voice he recognised, a voice he would never forget. He looked over and saw commander Yadav, the man who had shot his wife. Yadav seemed to be the only one in full control of his faculties, frustratedly yelling orders to the guards to get them formed into some sort of coherent fighting force, but who seemed to be incapable of following them.

Lutcher picked up an assault rifle from a dead guard, but then cast it aside as he made his way to the commander. Shooting Yadav would not be satisfying enough for him, he had to be close, he had to kill him with strength alone. Too late Yadav saw him, he tried to raise his weapon, but a hard blow to the side of his head stunned him and he collapsed to the ground. Lutcher put his foot on the man's throat.

"Her name was Sakami!" he yelled as he stamped down, bringing his whole weight to bear, crushing the man's throat. But in his rage he didn't see a guard taking aim at him.

Orlo saw it and threw a knife, killing the man, but not before he got a shot off, the bullet striking Lutcher across the shoulder. Orlo went to him, wiping some blood from a wound on his arm that he had sustained and pressed it onto Lutcher's wound.

"We are now blood brothers."

<<<<>>>>

Dhazi had just two more levels to go, three more bodies lay in his wake, all three killed with his bare hands, his rage giving him the strength to take them all on. Ahead he heard voices, two more, possibly three more guards. He glanced around a corner and saw three men, they seemed relaxed, casual, apparently unaware of what was happening outside. Two of them had even laid their weapons down.

He stepped out into the corridor and fired two shots, taking down two of the men. He went to fire again, but this gun was now empty. He chucked the gun to the side and charged at the man who was scrabbling to pick up his assault rifle. He body checked the man, with both falling to the ground, both reaching for the gun. Dhazi got there first, snatching it and pulled the trigger, but nothing happened.

He flipped the gun around to use it as a club and swung it at the man's head. The guard put his hands up defensively, but his movements were slow and did nothing to stop the butt of the weapon smashing into the side of his head. Over and over Dahzi rained down blows until he heard the man's skull crack and the futile defensive attempts stopped. He left the man, there was just one more level to go.

The final guard station was empty, and again, all the CCTV screens were blank. Only one set of steps was between him and his ultimate goal. He made his way up, but cautiously this time, he was so close, but his rage had not diminished. Once again he thought of Ayeka and his sense of determination redoubled in his mind.

He entered the corridor, ahead was the door to the penthouse. He moved cautiously, his knife in his hand. Suddenly, two praetorian guards stepped out in front of him. He lunged at them, his knife having no effect on their armour. A blow to the side of his head sent him to the ground, and a kick to his hand sent his knife clattering away. Another two guards piled on top of him as his hands were pulled behind his back and shock cuffs slapped on. He cried out as an agonising charge of electricity surged through his body making him fully aware of how futile any resistance would be.

Meeting Calder.

Calder dismissed the guards and looked down on the young rebel strapped into a chair. "So, we finally meet, the rebel that wants me dead."

"You killed Ayeka," hissed Dhazi through clenched teeth. "I swore on that day that I would find a way to get to you and kill you."

"Ah yes, the flame thrower. Well, technically I didn't kill her."

"You gave the order, you must have said how she was to die." Dhazi shouted as he lunged forward as far as the restraints would allow. "So you are responsible."

"Hmm." Calder smirked, ignoring the bluster of the young man. "From the information I received, your girlfriend was the one that came up with the idea of dissolving plastic in solvent, so when the firebomb exploded burning fuel would stick to whoever was unfortunate enough to be caught in the blast." He turned to Dhazi, a sarcastic sneer on his face. "So you could say I was just fighting fire with fire."

Anguish came over Dhazi as he remembered seeing her. "She was twenty-one, I found her body burned beyond all recognition."

"You found 'a' body, and as you rightly say, it was burned beyond all recognition. So how do you know it was her?"

Dhazi paused, the fact that it might not have been Ayeka had not occurred to him before.

"No, it was her, she was wearing the necklace and ring that I gave her."

Calder sat down, smug in the knowledge that he had sown enough anger and confusion in the young man's head, and it was now time to tell him the truth.

"There was a wastrel, a girl, dead on the street from whatever reason, maybe it had been a hit and run, who knows. She was perfect, she was about the same size as your girlfriend and looked a lot like her. My men were ready and waiting in the 'safe' house. Ayeka was caught and the ring and necklace taken from her, it was put on whoever this girl was, then she was taken away and the already dead girl got a blast from a flame thrower, and I made sure that it was witnessed by your friend Hyodo."

Calder stopped and frowned at the confused young man strapped into the chair. "I'm not a complete monster. Your girlfriend is alive and well in a penal colony on the other side of Matrea. Not the most comfortable place to be, but at least she's alive..." He paused and looked into Dhazi's eyes seeing the relief and joy that the news that momentarily overrode the situation he was in. "... at least she's alive and unharmed.

"The screams were a recording. You didn't notice the playback device when you found what you thought was your girlfriends corpse, why would you? Your focus was on her, and if you'd have looked closely, you'd have seen the ring that you gave her was on the wrong finger. That was a test I set up, and I knew right then that you believed it to be Ayeka and I had you exactly the way I wanted you."

Dhazi sat confused with his feelings, joy that his girlfriend was alive, but angry that he had been fooled in such a callous way. "Why did you do that?"

"I needed you to be angry enough to work out a way of getting in. I knew when you would come; I knew the date and the time, so I scheduled system-wide maintenance of the security cameras which is why all of them were down. I altered the patrol timings. I made sure that some of the guard's weapons were faulty and would misfire. I made sure that their magazines were either not full or empty. I also had those guards drugged so that their reactions were slower, and they would be significantly weaker, making them easier for you to kill.

"I fomented the notion of dissent within the security forces and incompetence within the palace, which you believed and is the reason why you didn't raise any questions when found some doors unlocked and guard stations unattended. This was intended to guide you to me, and it worked, didn't it? But most importantly, I relied on your youthful over-confidence that would make you think it was your skill that enabled you to overcome the obstacles in your way. All the guards were ordered to take you alive, regardless of the risks to themselves. The last four hadn't been drugged which is why you couldn't overpower them."

"You sacrificed your own men?" gasped Dhazi.

"But of course. When they sign up to serve as

palace guards, they agree to be used in any way that I deem fit, and that means that if I decide that they are to die at the hands of a twenty-one year old then so be it. They didn't realise they would die at your hand, they assumed it would be in some glorious fight to defend me."

"How did you know what time I'd come?"

"Oh Dhazi, you are so young and idealistic, not yet polluted with the cynicism that age and experience brings. How do you think I knew? Could it have been my drone technology? Was it the surveillance cameras tracking you and alerting me to your activities? But most importantly, why was it that you, Ayeka and Hyodo were never harassed?"

A wave of doubt flooded through Dhazi as he thought of all the things that had happened and the assumptions he had made. "No," he gasped, shaking his head as the uncomfortable thoughts swirled inside him. "No, they couldn't..." his voice trailed away, and his doubt showed his realisation of what must have happened.

Calder looked at Dhazi with an almost fatherly expression as he watched the young man struggling with his thoughts. "If it's any consolation, it wasn't Ayeka, her loyalty to you is absolute, and that is something I am relying on."

A sickening feeling hit Dhazi, the only possible explanation was that Hyodo, his closest friend, the friend he'd had all his life, had betrayed him.

"No, not Hyodo it can't be," he gasped, not wanting

to believe the only possible explanation.

"Yes, Hyodo Simu had been working for me for a while now." Calder handed over a sheet of paper with Hyodo's distinctive handwriting on it. "Here's the letter he sent me."

Dear Leader.

My name is Hyodo Simu. My parents are sick, they will die without medicine. They have run out of money and thought they were entitled to free medication, but they missed an appointment and now the hospital is refusing to give it to them. The administrator sent a letter saying that they don't qualify anymore, and they can't afford to pay for a private prescriptions.

Please, I am begging you to help them. If you do, I will do anything you ask, absolutely anything.

Durie and Li-soo are their names, please don't let them die. My life will be yours if you save them.

Thank you.

Hyodo Simu.

"I'd become aware of your activities and what better way to find out more than through inside information. I had him brought here and did a deal. Look at the date."

A chill ran through the young man. The date was a week before the special security police attack that killed Ellie and the others. Calder saw the revulsion on Dhazi's face. "They thought he was their friend," he gasped, breathless with anger.

Calder smirked. "Yes, and what better way to test his new loyalty to me."

Dhazi thought back to that day. Everyone was killed, but Hyodo managed to escape with what now seemed like a token injury.

Calder saw the recognition on Dhazi's face as the young man's expression hardened, an expression that quickly turned to disgust. "He worked for you, he betrayed everyone's trust, he provided information that got people killed, people who thought he was their friend. And yet you had him arrested, tried as a traitor and executed, I watched him die. Is that how you treat everyone who works for you, pawns to be disposed of when they have fulfilled their purpose, like the guards?"

Calder said nothing, he just tapped a button and an image of a young man shuffling along a street was shown. He appeared hunched, his head hung low as he shuffled into a shop. A feed from the shop's camera showed his face, it was Hyodo, he looked gaunt and haggard.

Dhazi's jaw dropped open at the sight of his one-time friend. "But his trial was televised, and his execution was televised, I watched him being hanged."

"No, he acted the part quite well, and as for the 'executed' prisoner, did you see his face? Hyodo is broken now, destroyed by what he did, but don't think too harshly of him. He did what he had to do to save his family."

"But he didn't save them, did he? they died because they couldn't afford the medication."

Calder shook his head. "You still don't understand it do you? They didn't die, the coffins you saw going into the crematorium were empty."

"No, that's a lie," shouted Dhazi. "I know Hyodo, those tears were real."

Calder sneered. "But what should be obvious to you now, is that you *didn't* know Hyodo, did you?" he snarled. "When he rested his head on your shoulder those tears were tears of shame, shame at the revulsion he felt for himself. Shame at all the things I had told him he had to do if he wanted his parents to live." Calder paused and looked hard at Dhazi for a few moments, then sneered again. "Why do you think he was so upset when my special security police killed your pathetic little gang? Do you really think it was survivor's guilt when he said he should have died with them, that he deserved to die? No it was guilt because he told me where you were going to meet. He told me afterwards that he even tried to tell you about his future betrayals. He said that he kept saying that he deserved to die, but you dismissed it as shock." Calder Scoffed. "And why do you think he was so upset when he told you of Ayeka's death, why do you think he is so broken now?"

Dhazi thought back to the day Hyodo came to him and told him of Ayeka's death. The howling anguish from him, and despite his own anguish, he'd had to comfort his friend. He remembered that Hyodo had cried for two days and was not the same afterwards. Calder saw the realisation dawn on the young man.

"Yes, that's right, he thought then and he still thinks that he is responsible for her being burned alive. He knew that my men were waiting for her, they got in with a key supplied by him. He'd taken your key, had it copied and gave it to me. He thought she was going to be captured, which is actually what happened, but he doesn't know that. She was given a shot to silence her. I told him not to enter the building and to make some excuse to walk away. So he didn't see her being carried out. He saw the flames, he heard screams and he saw a body on fire. His imagination filled in the rest. Your girlfriend thinks that Lutcher betrayed you."

He paused to let Dhazi think about everything he had just learned and saw the confused emotions on the young man's face.

Calder scoffed. "You'd be surprised at what people will agree to do to protect the ones they love. Hyodo agreed to work for me in return for his parents being taken abroad and treated. I told him that as long as he kept doing what I told him, his parents would receive the medication they needed. After Ayeka's 'death' he came to me and said he couldn't do it anymore, but his parents are cured, and even though you think I am a liar, I'm not, I am a man of my word. I released him from his obligation, and after the fake trial and execution he was sent to live with his parents. It was just another element in my plan to get you to come to me."

"Why me?"

"You are central to my plan."

"Why didn't you just arrest me then? Why go through all of that?"

"Oh no, no, no, that would have never done. So many people are arrested every day, one more would have been insignificant. No, you needed to be seen as a fearless hero, the saviour of Matrea filled with a righteous indignation, battling your way in and confronting me."

"What?" gasped Dhazi incredulously.

"I spotted your talent years ago and I've been keeping my eye on you ever since. I saw that you were not like the other kids. You didn't get subsumed into the world of trivia, that I allow, the vapid pop-culture that softens the brains of the young. No, you had a healthy interest in sport, particularly motorbike racing. Your hero was Soto, but you didn't go along to race meetings in the hope of seeing a crash, like everyone else seemed to. Instead you were interested in winners, and there's no question that Soto was the greatest winner of all time."

There was a strange inflection in Calder's voice, a sort of mild mocking, but his expression remained inscrutable, leaving Dhazi confused as to where this conversation was heading. Calder shrugged sarcastically. "It was a shame that Soto died, but I couldn't let him live."

The young man was speechless for a couple of seconds. "You had him killed!" he finally managed to blurt out.

"Yes, he was getting far too popular and had made noises about going into politics. He's far more famous dead than he ever was alive, if that's even possible, but that fame can't be used against me now. People can only speculate on what he might have achieved.

"I pressured his chief engineer to plant a small device on the bike, that was quite easy, he needed money for a gambling debt. He thought it was a data logger, he didn't know it was an explosive that would detonate as soon as Soto got over four-hundred kilometres an hour. It wasn't supposed to take out his only rival, Matti, but that worked in my favour." Calder sat back, a curious, conceited expression on his face. "It's a shame his engineer committed suicide," he jeered, mockingly. "It meant he wasn't able to tell anyone about the device."

"You had him murdered and it made to look like suicide."

"But of course."

Dhazi sat speechless as he thought of how his admiration of Soto had been damaged by the incessant speculation of his abilities and the suggestions that he cheated in every race. Now he knew that the man had been honourable and his faith in him was restored.

"You had a man killed so that he couldn't ever depose you?"

"Yes, and not for the first time."

"He was a good man," shouted Dhazi.

"Yes, he was a good man. An honourable man, a decent man, modest and generous. A man with great dignity."

"All the qualities you hate," sneered Dhazi.

"No. They are all the qualities I admire. All the qualities that I wish I had but can never have. You see, Soto was popular, people would have rallied to him and yes, he might have even won and become Prime Minister. But I'll tell you what the problem with populist leaders is; they promise this, and they promise that. They say they're going to make everyone's life better once elected. For a while they do, and people love them for that. But the electorate only ever think short-term and sooner or later a difficult decision has to be made, and as with all political decisions, some people will lose out. Then the hero is not so shiny anymore.

"Take the idiot that thinks he's in charge at the moment, him with the bouffant haircut. He'll be out soon, no doubt replaced with someone wearing flamboyant clothes and with no clue as to what the job actually entails.

"I tolerate these imbeciles because they suit my purpose, and when they don't, or when they get too big for their boots, I sow division within their ranks." Calder smirked. "You may be too young to have noticed, but since I've ruled, no prime minister has ever served a full term, they've always been ousted by their own party. But Soto may have been different, he wouldn't have had a political party behind him with all the attendant internecine trauma, skulduggery and backstabbing that I create and encourage. He would have had the people behind him. He could have been a real threat to me. So he had to die.

"I had to let it go right to the wire so that he would die in the most spectacular way and with the greatest possible publicity, thereby ensuring his fame as a great rider and not as a politician. I didn't know it would be so close to the finish, that was a bonus. And yes, I spread the rumours of cheating to polarise opinion."

"Why? what possible motive could you have for that?"

"Distraction. While the media is filled with endless speculation over his death, nobody is taking notice of what's really going on. Even after all these years, I still drip feed rumours to the gullible to make sure that the story is kept alive." Calder scoffed a half-laugh. "Alive, that's an ironic use of the word."

There was a moment of silence as Calder stared out over Matrea, seemingly deep in thought. He turned back to face Dhazi.

"Soto brought a new level of dignity to the sport, he took a sport of ruffians and ennobled it, he made it respectable. Instead of bad-mouthing his opponents, he praised them, pointing out their skills. In interviews he would always name-check those riders he admired and would talk about them and not himself. People began to believe that modesty is a virtue, and it is.

"Now look at the sport, it's back to where it always was. Safety rules have been relaxed and people go along hoping to see a crash. Female riders have entered the sport now and their races are little more than pornography, with the girls wearing as little as possible. It's so low brow. There are nicely choreographed fake catfights before the races and well-rehearsed 'wardrobe malfunctions' as the winner stands on the podium." He paused and sneered. "Don't you find it strange that the camera is always in exactly the right position at exactly the right time when breasts are 'accidentally' exposed? Pathetic, isn't it?" Calder shrugged. "But still, the viewing figures are up, track day attendances are also up and the populous anesthetised, the pain of their existence dulled by the asinine spectacle."

He looked hard at Dhazi. "But you, you were different. You didn't seem to be going along with the crowd, you stood out, at least to me you did. I thought to myself *'this boy could be a leader'* so I've been watching you, moulding you into the person I need you to be. Now, take your mother and father, Erik and Kari. They've been harassed like everyone else, but there's never been any violence towards your father, and no abuse of your mother, verbal maybe, but nothing physical that other woman have to put up with."

"Am I supposed to thank you?"

"No, you're supposed to be angry. But here's where I was clever, had I allowed your father to be beaten up or your mother raped, then your anger would be focussed on getting revenge for them. Instead you heard stories from your friends about the abuse their parents had faced. You developed an angry contempt for me, but it was tinged with guilt that your family had been spared the full horror that I can unleash. Guilt is a powerful driver, and you wanted revenge for *their* families, not yours. Because it was not an immediate reaction to avenge your parents, you took the time to build a movement, a movement of the young. And you succeeded."

Dhazi tugged angrily at the restraints. "Let me out of this chair and I will kill you and put an end to your evil reign. I will make it quick, and I won't gloat over your death."

"Hmm," grunted Calder. "I am going to release you, but you will never get close enough to harm me, and by the time I have finished, you won't want to harm me. In fact you will want my dynasty to continue."

Dhazi sneered. "Okay, let me out and we'll see." Anger still boiled inside him as he thought of all the things Calder had crowed about, Hyodo's treachery, Soto being murdered, and the cruel trick making him believe that Ayeka had been burned to death. He still wasn't sure if Calder was lying about her, but he had no reason to lie, and Dhazi desperately wanted her to be alive.

Calder sighed. "Why does the youth of this land always want to do things the hard way?"

"You make it easy," snarled Dhazi as he tugged at the restraints again.

Calder ignored the sneering distain, it was what he expected.

"Every cubic millimetre of this space is scanned a thousand times a second. Every movement is tracked and analysed. Threats are assessed within a micro-second an appropriate action is taken. You will not be able to get within three metres of me, and you will not be able to throw anything or make any sort of threatening gesture." He pointed to devices in the ceiling. "If you do, this will happen." Calder pressed a button.

Dhazi cried out as an energy beam struck his leg, burning the top layer of his skin.

"It's a superficial burn and won't leave a scar because it was on less than a tenth of one per cent power. Any move against me will result in a one hundred per cent burn to your head. It's instant, speed of light stuff, so you won't be able to heroically dive out of the way. The beam will penetrate your skull and the heat will instantly boil the water in your brain; you'll be dead before you hit the floor. But don't worry, strangely, there aren't any pain sensors in the brain, and you won't briefly feel something on the surface of your head, because it will be all over for you instantly, and faster than your brain can register pain."

Calder, confident of his safety, held his hand over a button on his chair. "I am going to release you now, but you must be aware that there won't be a warning shot, the next shot *will* kill you. Which will be a shame because it will undo all the work I have done."

The restraints snapped open. "What do you mean, the work you have done?" grunted Dhazi as he rubbed his wrists to ease the discomfort. Calder dodged the question.

"Let me tell you about Matrea as it was forty generations ago."

Dhazi sneered. "The Matrea that your dynasty destroyed."

Calder sat back, a smug expression on his face. "So you believe the old legend of the glorious Matrean utopia, do you?"

"Yes," snapped Dhazi.

"That's just as well because it's all true."

"What?"

"Yes, going back a thousand years Matrea was a beacon of hope for all civilizations, a shining example of peace and prosperity that my ancestors brough to an end."

Dhazi sat aghast at the notion. "Why? Why would they want to put an end to it?"

Again, Calder ignored the question as he stood up and went to the window. He sighed as he looked out over Matrea, his realm. To the east, in the distance, smoke was rising from yet another riot. He couldn't hear the sirens through the soundproofed glass, but he could see the blue flashes of the armoured personnel carriers of the riot squads speeding towards the sector.

He turned back to face Dhazi, then gestured towards the East Zone "The riot squads have a quota to fill, they have been instructed to kill three rioters and no more, it doesn't matter how many they wound. The rest will be taken into custody and beaten. Then for the next week, punishment teams will go into the east sector and make examples of people. Old or young, male or female, it won't matter, one person chosen at random will be taken every day and will receive a very public beating."

"They have a kill quota?" gasped the young man.

"Oh yes, the rumours are true, all over Matrea, a certain number of people have to die every day and not enough have died today, if they had, then no-one else would need be killed. I have just found out that three more babies were born than were expected, so three more deaths are required."

Dhazi sat stunned and momentarily speechless at the confirmation of what had always been suspected. Calder tapped a screen and a video feed from a drone appeared. It showed shock troops pouring out of the vehicles and opening fire on a crowd. Scores dropped to the ground as the bullets struck.

Calder turned to him and shrugged. "The police squads have a lottery every day as to who gets to make the kill shot. The rest have to agree to shoot-to-wound, anyone who makes an unagreed kill shot gets a beating back at the station."

Dhazi shook his head, unable to find the words to express his disgust. "That is monstrous, utterly inhumane," he finally managed to say.

"Yes, it is, but it keeps the police moral up and maintains the fear in the population. And you know, the girls are the best shots, there's just something about female determination, it's a quality in women that I have always admired. They don't hesitate, they don't question, there's no self-doubt; if they are ordered to shoot you in the leg, you'll get shot in the leg. If they are ordered to shoot you in the throat, then you'll get shot in the throat, and with not a second thought from them."

The image zoomed in on a body on the ground. "There, headshot to the face by the looks of it. One down two to go." He turned to Dhazi and saw the hate on his face. "I know what you're thinking, you're thinking that if you're quick enough then you could grab me and turn me, so the beam hits me. Well, that won't work, so don't bother trying." He turned back to the screen just as the image zoomed in on another dead body, four massive holes in the woman's chest.

"The drone is programmed to detect kill-shots and zoom in on them. It helps with training," he calmly mentioned. "It's quite a clever bit of coding" he muttered blithely.

"How can you be so casual about this, people are dying!"

"Simple, it has to happen, but there's only going to be one more."

With that, a man's head burst open. The squads carried on shooting but were hitting arms and legs. Calder closed the transmission.

Dhazi's breath was reduced to short panting, he had seen deaths before, he had killed before, but seeing these deaths that had been so coldly calculated got to him "Those people had families, loved ones, dependants, don't you care about that?"

Calder sneered. "Nobody forced them to riot, no wait, you did! You with your *'let's overthrow Calder'* message. Your *'we will force him to change'* message. You got them all hyped up, you stopped the gangs fighting each other and persuaded them to fight against me. They were killing enough people, but you put an end to all that, you left me no choice but to engineer situations so I could send in the squads. So their deaths are on you!"

Anger got the better of Dhazi. "No! you can't put that on me!" he shouted.

"Oh, but I can, and I will, and when I have finished, you will understand why." Calder sat back down and studied Dhazi for a few moments, feeling the visceral hate from the young man.

"A thousand years ago Matrea was wealthy, food was plentiful and cheap, everyone owned their own homes and there was space, plenty of elbow room, to put it crudely.

"There was clean water and few diseases to worry about. It had art, culture, music, and people were free to marry whomsoever they desired. There was no poverty. It was as near to perfect as it is possible to get, it was known as Matrea's golden age, and it lasted for five hundred years."

"Then your ancestors tore it down, why?" demanded Dhazi.

"Living conditions were perfect, everyone had

exactly what they needed, so people started to not bother doing any meaningful work. Pursuit of pleasure became uppermost in their minds. People indulged themselves to the full, whether it be physical, spiritual or sexual. They stopped going to work, the birth rate fell, those infants born were neglected by their mothers who were more interested in having a good time, rather than providing care for their offspring. People stopped getting married; after all, why should they when there was so much free time and so much fun and casual sex to have. The men that fathered children disregarded their progeny, seeing them as an impediment to whatever pleasure they were seeking.

"Then the brutes emerged, they called themselves *The Supremes*. Certain males grew much larger than all the others and would spend all their time either working out or preening, becoming ever more vain. Each of them would spend hours looking in mirrors admiring their own musculature. When they weren't doing that, they would band together showering complements on each other before marauding through towns, intimidating men who they saw as being weak and inferior.

"They had no interest in women, even though waif-like females would be drawn to them, freely offering any sexual favours they desired. But they rejected sex and desired only the company of other Supremes.

"Apathy was causing the whole society to collapse; nobody wanted to work in health care, and the birth rate was heading to a point where infant deaths outnumbered births. My ancestors were political scientists; they ran an experiment using mice, giving them perfect living conditions analogous to the human experience in Matrea. They ran the experiment with different species, and no matter how many times they ran the experiment, the results were always the same. Once the brutes appeared, the society would have gone past the point of no return and would fail, and *all* the animals would die. They predicted that Matrea would cease to exist within two generations unless something was done.

"The conclusion was obvious, humans need to struggle, they need something to aim for to better themselves and give their lives purpose. So my ancestors created the struggle to save the society."

Dhazi grunted contemptuously. "That is utterly absurd, all that may have been true back then, but not now."

"Oh, you think so? Let us do a little thought experiment. Rather than the violent overthrow that you attempted, let's say you somehow find your way into what passes for parliament and make an eloquent, impassioned speech that makes even my most ardent supporter question their loyalty to me. Let's say that senior generals arrest me and have me shot, then write a constitution that turns the country over to civilian rule. How long do you think it would be before all the old rivalries start to boil over, with Lutcher and Orlo at each other's throats again? I can assure you that you will end up with a Matrea far worse than you have now."

Dhazi shook his head defiantly. "No, that won't

happen, the Calder dynasty is a cancer ready to be plucked out. People will rejoice in your death and maybe we will be able to rebuild Matrea back to its former glory."

Calder chuckled and shook his head. "Oh the idealism of youth, so naïve, so lacking in experience of human nature. Just as a matter of interest, what was your plan for the economy once I was gone? No, let me guess, you didn't have one did you? I suppose you were going to 'work something out'. I'm right, aren't I?"

Dhazi was speechless, this was an aspect that he hadn't considered.

"I'll take your silence as a yes. Well let's say I got deposed, tried and executed. No doubt the first thing you, and by you, I mean the committee you'd form, the first thing you would announce is redevelopment. There'd be big civic works, new builds, updating of infrastructure etc... and you wouldn't have a clue how to pay for it."

"There would be plenty of people in the banking sector willing to help us."

"Yes, you're probably right. And the first thing they'd say is raise taxes. How popular would you be then?"

Dhazi sneered at him. "We'd have all your money."

"True, but that wouldn't get you far, it works out at around five thousand credits for every citizen, big deal! But what would happen after a year? Some people will have spent the money wisely, improving their home, investing for their children, or maybe even starting businesses. Then there'd be the other lot, squandering all their money on drink and gambling or frivolous pursuits, ending up with not enough money to live on. Then they'd come bleating to you wanting more, no, demanding more because 'It isn't fair'," he sneered. "You'd arrange a welfare payment system for them and then the ones who had used their money wisely would start bleating that it isn't fair.

"Or you could use the money for new motorway or two, new bridges to replace the crumbling ones. You could announce a big new housing project, all that would generate full employment and would keep the people happy... for a bit. But once you've started, the people will expect more and more, and you'd have to give them more or they'd say you were just like me, promising but not delivering. Then you'd have no choice but to raise taxes."

Calder pressed a button, and the screen showed a workstation in another room switching on. "That terminal will connect you to the most powerful quantum computer ever made. Go ahead, use it to predict the future after my regime has fallen. Run every simulation you can think of, run every permutation of every possible interaction. I can tell you what happens because I spend every day of my life doing it. I have run hundreds of thousands of simulations and the results are always the same. Everyone will be deliriously happy for six months, then egos will take over.

"Within two years there'll be a brutal six way civil war as each side believes that their plan is better and tries to impose it on the others."

"The Praetorian Guards, the Army, the Special Security Police, the Riot Police, the regular Police and your rabble will all have different ideas of how Matrea should be run. Alliances will change on a daily basis, there'll be an abundance of weapons freely available and there will be massacres, and as usual, the civilians will be the ones that suffer.

"But I suppose you'll insist on running the sims, so go ahead, take as much time as you need. You have full access to the population database and all police and military tactics, capabilities and doctrines. You can only run simulations, you can't issue orders or engage in cyber-sabotage or any other disruptive activities that I'm sure you'd love to do." He pressed a button and two guards entered. "Take him to room eight, and there's no need to be rough, just ensure he doesn't get away." The guards pulled Dhazi's hands behind his back, slapped on shock cuffs and led him away. Calder snapped his fingers to stop them.

"I'll have some food and water sent in, along with some cream and dressing for the burn on your leg. You'll eventually be taken back to a cell for the night, but I will make sure that it will be a comfortable one. As I have stated, run as many sims as you want, take as long as you want."

"Do you expect me to be grateful?"

"No, I expect you to be realistic about the future."

Calder waved them away then stopped them as they got to the door. "Oh and when you run the simulations, you'll see that in all of them there's a character labelled 'A1', that's you!"

<<<<>>>>

Dhazi sat back, shocked. Over the past four days, he'd run over three thousand simulations and Calder was correct. Each one predicted brutal civil wars, some that would last generations, with every conflict causing the deaths of untold numbers of civilians. In all of the simulations he survived but he always ended up becoming a dictator far worse than Calder ever was. He would order mass deportations and declare vast numbers of the populous as hostile agents and have them interred in overcrowded concentration camps where disease would run rampant. Matrea would break up into individual centres of power with each one trying to take over. Hunger would be used as a weapon by all sides as they attacked food production and distribution with himself being the chief protagonist of this tactic to starve out opposition to his rule.

Underground labs would emerge, manufacturing powerful, highly addictive synthetic drugs that stole the lives of kids like him. Families would be torn apart as parents became addicts, neglecting their children. Crime would skyrocket as homes and businesses were broken into by users desperate to find money or goods to steal and sell in order to maintain their habit. People would be mugged in broad daylight, daughters and maybe some sons would turn to prostitution to fund their addiction. Every sim that Dhazi ran to find a way of combatting the problem had him responding by reinstating the death penalty for anyone suspected of being a user.

But what disturbed him the most was that every one of the simulations showed Ayeka turning against him, and him having her branded as a traitor and thrown in prison, never to be released.

Dhazi had also run simulations that had Calder still in power and these shocked him more. In every single one, life for the citizens of Matrea stayed the same as it always had been, a daily struggle. The sims showed that some people would have more than they needed, but most would have only just enough. Lutcher's zone of influence would spread, Orlo would continue to run the south zone, and the two men would continue to send their minions to fight and kill each other. But there were no full scale civil wars, no massacres of civilians no mass slaughter in extermination camps, there was just enough food and there were no drugs.

On day five Calder entered the room alone. Dhazi stood up sharply, turned to him and pointed all around the room.

"I don't see any high energy beam emitters in here. That means I could kill you," he yelled, but doubt laced his voice, a doubt that Calder expected.

"But you're not going to, are you? because you've seen what will happen."

Dhazi sighed and sat down, putting his head in his hands. "Yes," he muttered into his chest, defeated by what he had seen.

"Now you understand, Matrea needs me."

Dhazi said nothing.

"I'll take your silence as an indication that you agree with me."Dhazi shook his head slightly, not in disagreement, but at himself for agreeing.

"After the first few simulations you thought to yourself that you knew the future and would take steps to avoid it. I am right, aren't I?"

"Yes."

"So you adjusted the parameters, but nothing changed the outcomes, did it?"

"No."

"No, nothing will, I learned that years ago. But what the simulations do show is that I need you, Dhazi Noran, and Matrea needs you."

Dhazi's head snapped up. "What do you need me for? I don't understand you."

"I need you to do something, something that will benefit everyone."

"What is it!" he demanded.

"I need you to keep doing what you are doing, organise rebellions, unite people and give them hope. Make them believe that I can be overthrown. Though for all the reasons you have seen, you will never be able to succeed."

"Why, what is the point?" shouted Dhazi. "You can crush any rebellion, that's why I started to fight back."

"Exactly!" shouted Calder. "That is precisely why I need you! The Matreans were getting lazy, idle, I would even go so far as saying they were slothful. Nobody was willing to stand up anymore and I was getting too powerful. Matrea was out of balance, then you came along, and I saw the qualities in you. You persuaded Lutcher and Orlo to make peace and fight against me, you drew teenagers away from the facile trivia that they had become addicted to, and it was then that I realised you would be the one to bring balance back."

"You are complaining about having too much power?" gasped Dahzi incredulously, unable to understand why this would be a problem for a dictator.

Calder gestured all around. "The people need balance, it is the only way that Matrea can survive, you saw that in the sims, and you know that it's true. I need you to fight against me, the people need you to fight against me."

"And if I say no?"

"Then Matrea will fall. I know you ran simulations with me staying in power, but you made a mistake, you assumed that I would stay as I am. I ran different sims, ones where my power continues to grow. In all of those sims, I eventually destroy Matrea. You see, I had a factor in my simulations that you didn't have in yours; a tiny invisible element. Every single Calder has had the same personality defect, it's genetic and it can't be altered; inactivity brings on megalomania, a manic desire for power at any cost. This gene that all Calder's' have follows a recessive pattern, it lays dormant and activates in every other generation; it's why my predecessor appeared so weak compared to his predecessor.

"Twenty years ago I was informed that the gene was now active in me, and the only way to keep it in check is through action. Have you not noticed that since you started your activities, there have been no new laws, yes rules have been tightened, decrees issued, but no new laws made. That was you doing that. Before you came along my 'condition' was starting to assert itself, but then you gave me something to focus on. If you keep me occupied then Matrea will survive."

"Matrea will survive but with the people oppressed and struggling. It would be pointless, it…"

"With you leading them!" interrupted Calder. "With you giving them hope, they'll always be looking forward to a better future."

"It will be a future without hope!" shouted Dhazi. "How can I lead them if I know there is no hope?"

"Only you and I will know that there is no hope, but there will be balance!" shouted Calder as he banged his fist on the table.

Dhazi sat down, emotions churning inside him as he thought about all the simulations he ran; the disastrous effect of him winning, and the results of the sims where Calder stayed in power. "There has to be another way," he muttered.

"There isn't," sighed Calder as he reached over to the keyboard and entered a code.

"This unlocks all my factors. Now run sims with me surviving."

Calder left the room, eight hours later he returned to find Dhazi with his head in his hands again.

"You understand now, don't you."

Dhazi said nothing and sat rubbing his forehead, knowing that his silence implied agreement.

"Do I have a choice?" he mumbled, unwilling to believe that he was going to be, in effect, a traitor, working with and for the very person he had sworn to kill.

"No you don't. If you really care for the people of Matrea, then you don't have a choice. I will guarantee your safety and the safety of your parents." Calder could see Dhazi's conflict and played the ace. He entered a code and a video from a prison canteen appeared. Dhazi couldn't avoid letting out a whimper as he saw Ayeka alive and well sitting at a table, eating. Another girl approached and started shouting at her. Ayeka stood up and squared off against the girl, the altercation lasted a few seconds before guards intervened.

Calder paused the image and pointed to the other girl. "This was recorded yesterday. In about five days' time, a situation will be engineered where the female will start a fight with Ayeka. I know how tough your girlfriend is, she will win, but the girl will die. Ayeka won't kill her; the girl will be injected with something when she gets to the infirmary, but your girlfriend will be accused of her murder. She will be tried, found guilty and executed."

Dhazi fully realised what this meant. "If I don't agree," he snarled.

"Yes, if you don't agree, your girlfriend will be hanged or shot, I haven't quite made up my mind yet. Is that motivation enough?"

"You utter bastard!"

Calder dismissed the insult with a wave of his hand.

Dhazi stood up and stared hard at Calder, options running through his mind. "I want Ayeka freed, and I want her safety guaranteed as well."

"I won't free her, but I can arrange the conditions for you to rescue her."

Dhazi struggled with the conflict inside, pacing back and forth as he tried to reason with himself. Eventually he stopped and turned to Calder. "If I agree, *will* you guarantee her safety?"

"Yes."

"You say that you are a man of your word. How do I know you'll keep your word?"

"I will, I hold all the cards, so I have no need or reason to lie."

Dhazi stared at the floor for a few moments, he sat down and hung his head, defeated. "Then I agree."

"Good, we have an understanding. And now you

know what I meant when I said you'd be surprised at what people will agree to do to protect the ones they love."

"That was your plan all along, wasn't it?"

"Yes. I wasn't one hundred percent sure that I could persuade you and needed to give you one final push."

"Would you have gone through with it? Would you have allowed her to be executed?"

"Yes."

Dhazi stood up and paced around, trembling, unable to fully come to terms with the situation he found himself in but knew that Calder had no reason to lie. Emotions churned inside him, making his head swim as he first thought she had died a hideous death, then found out that she was alive and then had the threat of her execution if he didn't agree to the dictator's terms.

Calder could sense the turmoil in the young man and his agitated state. He let him take a few minutes to calm down.

"I will arrange for your escape later today. I will erase all records relating to you, no-one in the palace knows your name, all that people will know is that the leader of the rebellion was captured but managed to escape after a few days due to the incompetence of the guards." Calder smirked sarcastically, "That should enhance your standing with your followers and maybe imbue you with a touch of charisma. You'll be a hero."

Calder let his words sink in for a few moments. "You need to think of yourself as a military leader and there is an odd aspect to the human psyche. Charismatic leaders can order their followers into situations where there is certainty of death, the followers willingly do it and some get killed. But instead of the survivors resenting the leader, their respect for them is often enhanced. As the reputation spreads more people are drawn to fight for him despite the obvious risk of death. Odd, don't you think?"

Again, Calder let his words sink in. "The trick for you will be to make sure the right number of your people die, too many and your followers will turn against you, not enough and your leadership abilities will be questioned. You can't have people die in every operation, but there will need to be at least one in every other action you take against me. I don't care how many of my people you kill and I will ensure that there are always more deaths on my side than yours, that will enhance your leadership reputation."

Dhazi said nothing. Instead a shiver ran down his spine as he realised the full implication of what the man was saying.

"You will be taken to a cell and a few things will be left there for you to use tonight." Calder smirked. "I will give you a knife. You will kill a guard with it then take his weapon and fight your way out of the palace." Dhazi shuddered slightly as he heard the same words that Orlo had used, only changing 'into' for 'out of', confirming that Calder had heard every word that had been said in the flat. "You will need to kill no more than

THE COLLABORATOR

one other person, too many and people will smell a rat –
which is what you are now!"

A medical orderly entered the room pushing a
trolly with various needles, cannulae and syringes.
Dhazi looked at them in horror. "What are they for?"

"Don't worry, it's nothing sinister. Your story will
be that you had been injected with truth drugs but
resisted for four days before heroically escaping. I have
started the rumour that only those with exceptional
willpower and courage can resist the effect of the drug,
but you need some injection sites. Hold your arms out."

Dhazi dismissed his fears about getting a lethal
injection, it would be an overly elaborate way to kill
him, when a single shot from a guard was all that was
needed. He did what he was told, flinching as needles
pierced the skin in the crook of his elbow. Canulae were
inserted into the backs of his hands then drawn out
and dressings applied. The orderly left them.

"Obviously, you will need to remove the dressings
before you escape." Calder sneered slightly. "You don't
want people to think that your time here was
comfortable, do you?"

"What about Ayeka?" snapped Dhazi.

"As I said, I won't free her, even I have to play by the
rules… sometimes." A picture of a couple of unpleasant
looking prison guards appeared. Your girlfriend is
scheduled to be transferred to another prison in two
days' time. These men, Sergeants Saekki and Kai-aal
will take her. They are suspected of being serial rapists
who are thought to take a, let's call it a scenic route, and

have a specific spot where they stop to do what they like to do. I know where that is. I will give you the location and the time; a weapon will be left there for you. What you do with it is up to you.

"The women always complain about the sexual abuse but are not believed, because, well, they are criminals whose word cannot be trusted. Those who have visible bruises have their complaints dismissed when the men say that the women offered them sex and said they liked it rough. Because they are both Sergeants and have spent years in service they are believed, and the women are not."

Calder frowned slightly. "You may find this strange but
of all the things you despise me for, sexual abuse of women actually disgusts me, and I've been wanting a way to get rid of these two for a while. Their death by you will further serve my purpose."

Dhazi sneered incredulously at the dictator. "And yet you allow some women to be raped."

Calder waved his hand dismissively. "Simple tactics. It's just like the leaders who send their followers to certain death. They don't like giving the orders, but it's just a tactic in the overall strategy. It's something that you need to learn and learn quickly.

"Now, back to the matter in hand. There will be losses on both sides, and this is something that you'll just have to accept. You will see friends die, comrades cut down before their life has even begun. The first few times it happens it will undoubtedly upset you, you may even have a breakdown at some point, but it will get easier as time goes on." Calder fixed a hard stare on Dhazi. "This is your reality now." He paused to let his words fully sink in, then shrugged. "I will lose men, but none of them are important to me. So take my advice, you can stay close to Ayeka, but don't get close to anyone else. Lutcher and Orlo's men will die, and as a concession to you, and to make your task a touch easier, I will make sure that these troops bear the brunt of the deaths, that will be useful to you.

"Retribution will obviously have to be taken against the populous, though it will not be a severe as before. That will make people believe that you are having successes, they will think I am wary of stirring up anger. I will ensure that the two principal commanders in your rebel army, Orlo and Lutcher, are not killed, though they *will* have to get injured.

"History is filled with military leaders that have lost an arm or a leg and have gone on to inspire their troops to victory, and that will be useful to me." Calder paused and scoffed. "I will allow you to have some small victories, you will take positions and hold them for a while, you will seem to be making progress but will eventually be driven back." He glowered down at Dhazi, the menace in his eyes plain to see. "The struggle will be constant, as will the deaths."

Dhazi looked up at Calder, his disgust visceral. "I hate you so much," he snarled.

Calder waved his hand dismissively. "What you think of me is irrelevant. The knife and the other items will be under your mattress, make your move at ten tonight."

"I feel sick."

"That is understandable, but you can hide your self-loathing behind the loathing that you feel for Hyodo and your disgust at the way your best friend betrayed you. Don't worry though, as with the deaths, it will get easier with time. You will eventually come to see people for what they are, just disposable tools for you to use for the greater good of Matrea. You have to understand that from now on they are not your friends, and you are not theirs."

"I am a collaborator," grunted Dhazi, disgusted with himself. "I'm no better than Hyodo."

Calder shook his head and seemed confused. "No, this is not a collaboration, it is an alliance."

"I don't see it that way."

"As you wish, but you know that this is the only way forward if *we* are to save Matrea, there are no other paths."

Dhazi shook his head sorrowfully; Calder was right, this was the only way forward.

"You and I will never meet again, but I will be aware of your actions, just as I was aware of the bug above the table that some of my men use; I gave it to Hyodo to give to you. My men have loose lips when they are drunk, and I will get information to you via them." Calder smirked conceitedly. "I knew exactly what your plans were because that was not the only bug I gave Hyodo. I don't need it anymore, so as a mark of good faith, I'll tell you where it is. It's in an electrical socket, the one near the table where you sat and made your plans. The one that was allegedly broken and that Hyodo replaced. It transmits an encrypted signal directly to me. It's not a video camera, I'm not a voyeur."

Cold shot through Dhazi's veins at this further betrayal. The thought that Calder had listened to everything that happened in that room was almost too much. There was just the two of them in the room, and despite every fibre of his being screaming at him to attack Calder, he knew he couldn't. Not just because he had to save Ayeka, but because of what the sims had predicted. He had seen all the possible futures, and this vile deal that he had agreed to was the only way of saving Matrea.

Escape.

Calder had laid out everything that was to happen, every move that Dhazi was to make. There would be three items in the cell, a knife, and exit permit and a set of car keys, all under the mattress.

Dhazi's anger had blinded him to what was really happening when he fought his way into the palace five days ago. He had assumed, as Calder pointed out, that it was his skill that enabled him to battle his way through. His confidence had grown with every man he killed. His belief in the incompetence of the palace guards had increased with every door he found unlocked and every guard station empty. Now he knew that all those men had been unwitting pawns, assets to be disposed of as part of Calder's perverse plan to save Matrea.

He was a pawn too, though given all that Calder had said, he was fairly certain he wasn't one of the disposable pawns. It was eight in the evening and he had been put in a different cell, an underground cell, but one that was closer to the rear of the palace. The door slammed shut behind him and he stood for a moment disgusted at what he was going to have to do in a couple of hours' time. His motivation to kill had been easy as he fought hisway in, now he knew that motivation had been cruelly engineered. Ayeka wasn't dead, but she would be abused if he didn't do what he had been told, of that he was certain.

He took the items from under the mattress he stared at the knife. It was big, he felt the edge, it was razor sharp. He held it, feeling its balance, and all the while wondering if he really could go through with it but knowing that he had to.

There was no window, no clock and no sense of time passing. He heard someone coming, it could have been fifteen minutes since he was put in the cell but guessed that he must have been in there for about an hour. He quickly hid the knife, but was confused, Calder had said to make his escape at ten, but two hours couldn't have passed. The door opened and a guard entered with some food and water. Though wearing the intimidating body armour, he wasn't stern or angry looking, instead his expression was neutral, almost friendly.

The guard left the cell, locked it, then peered in through a grille. "Enjoy your meal. I'll be back in an hour, got to take you to another cell."

Dhazi instantly felt nauseous. This was obviously the man he was supposed to kill, a despicable scenario set up by Calder to test him. If he did not go through with it, then any of the scenarios could come true. He thought of Ayeka and the fate that awaited her, a fate that he had to alter. Over the course of the next hour he resigned himself to the task, as he knew that if he didn't do exactly as Calder had instructed, then he would never leave the palace. His girlfriend would be raped, and knowing the way she would fight them, she might even be killed. And then all of Matrea would fall through Calder's totalitarianism.

He put the keys and the exit permit in his pocket, then looked at the food; he didn't want it, though he knew he had to eat to get his strength up. He ate most of the meal and just about managed to keep it down, though the water was the most important thing, so he drank all of that.

His stress levels rose as the hour passed, and he hoped that he would be mentally strong enough for the task. Finally he heard the key in the door and the metallic clank of the bolts drawing back. Dhazi stood up, got the knife and held it behind his back. He needed to do it now and would need to be quick, as he knew that any hesitation would give him time to think, and then he might not go through with it. The guard entered and walked towards Dahzi, ending up just a metre away. He seemed unsteady on his feet, his eyes hollow, his expression blank. He also had a gun, a pistol in a holster which was something he didn't have before. Dhazi thought back to when Calder had shown him this type of weapon, how to handle it and how to load the magazine, and how to fire the gun. He remembered just how easy it would have been to have just shot Calder, there and then. But he hadn't, Calder knew he wouldn't.

The man was wearing a shirt, and not the body armoured tunic he was wearing earlier, that had a high stiff collar designed to protect the neck. Dhazi needed this man's death to be quick and quiet; he remembered how Orlo killed Di-aal and his words afterwards.

"Come on," mumbled the guard.

It was now or never. Dhazi whipped the knife across the man's throat but didn't cut as deep as Orlo had struck Di-aal. Blood immediately began to pump out from the guards' severed carotid artery and jugular vein, but his strike hadn't gone all the way across, and he hadn't penetrated the man's trachea. The man could have screamed, but didn't seem to react, his hands stayed down by his side, but he did open his mouth, and Dhazi didn't know if he would scream or not, so he took a swing back, this time harder and aiming deeper. But the man had started to sink to his knees and instead of the veins and arteries, he slashed deep into the man's cheek and mouth, opening it up, exposing the man's lower jaw as he collapsed to the ground.

Blood pumped from the cuts to his neck, foaming out of his mouth and bubbling out of the flap of flesh hanging down from his jaw. The man was lying on his back, his eyes wide open, and he didn't seem to be aware that he was injured and about to die. He didn't even have the natural reaction of putting his hands to the wounds to try and stem the flow. He rolled his head and stared at Dhazi.

Standing over his victim, and with blood dripping off the blade, Dhazi knew the man had been drugged and realised that he wasn't feeling any pain. Though Dhazi couldn't stand the disturbing, oblivious look on the dying man's face and had to finish him off. He dropped down then slammed the knife into the man's chest, all the way up to the hilt, then dived to the sink and threw up.

He sat back on the bed, looking down at the dead body, shocked and stunned at what he had just done, but realised that he now didn't have much time. He took the guard's side-arm, checked that the magazine was full and left the cell. Calder said that he was to kill one more, any less and it might be suspicious, too many would also be suspicious. There would be no official report of the escape, but Calder would allow a rumour to immediately spread. His logic was that by only killing two, Dhazi would come across as restrained and compassionate, qualities that would draw more people to him.

Dhazi remembered the layout and made his way along corridors and up to the ground level, heading to the rear of the palace and on towards the jetty. All the corridors were empty, guard stations were unattended, doors were blocked open. This was Calder's doing, exactly as it had been five days ago. Though this time there were no guards to fight - yet.

He was one turn away from the exit and could already hear water lapping against the banks of the river. He turned a corner to see the doors open and a guard facing way from him. He froze momentarily, this was the other person he had to kill. Weapon raised and ready, he made his way towards the man, but his hands were shaking and he needed to get closer to guarantee a hit. He crept forward as silently as possible, all the time wondering if he should make a noise at the last moment to make the man turn so that he wouldn't have to shoot him in the back.

Dhazi considered making a sound which would get their attention, that way killing him could be self-defence. He was three metres from the man and had his weapon lined up on the centre of his back. Three shots; Calder had said he had to hit the man with three shots to make it convincing. He steeled himself, his finger tightening on the trigger when a door slammed behind him, but the guard didn't respond, didn't turn to see what it was. It was clear that this man had also been drugged.

A wave of anguish came over him as he pulled the trigger three times and saw three holes rip open the man's back, the force throwing him forward with him ending up face down, killed as the bullets fragmented and tore his heart to shreds. Ten more metres saw Dhazi out of the palace and onto the jetty. As promised, there was a small boat, its electric motor meaning he would make a swift but silent getaway. He now had less than thirty-six hours to save Ayeka.

Calder watched the video feed of Dhazi getting into the boat, starting the motor and making his way downstream and out of shot, he had watched the entire escape on CCTV.

"Well done boy," he muttered as he hit 'Delete', erasing the recordings.

The riots were quelled, the people subdued, order restored. But the riots that had spontaneously broken out gave Dhazi a strange comfort, as it proved to him that people were willing to stand up to Calder. It gave him comfort, but it shouldn't have done, he was conflicted because people would be drawn to him and the fight would continue and some of those people would have to die.

He made his way home, ditching the boat and ducking through side alleys to stay out of sight of the police. He was ninety-nine percent certain that Calder had erased his records, but that remaining one percent told him to avoid the police if he could, and he knew this feeling would haunt him forever. He briefly debated contacting Lutcher and Orlo but decided against it, right now, Ayeka's rescue was far more important.

He gathered some of her clothes then carefully made his way to the location where Calder had told him the car would be waiting for him, a car that he said had no tracking device. Dhazi had no choice but to believe him.

A Rescue.

Dhazi tensed as he approached the checkpoint. He was on the main road and there were just a few more meters to go before he was out of the city. He worried that this might be some sort of convoluted plan by Calder that would have him get a bullet or two in the back as he passed through from the assault weapon proudly displayed in the window. A plan that would have him labelled as a dangerous terrorist killed while fleeing in a stolen car. But so far everything was as Calder said it would be. The escape, though unpleasant, was easy and the car was exactly where he said it would be, keys in it, the tank full of fuel and an envelope with a thousand credits on the seat.

He would tell Ayeka that he stole the car and the money. He would say that for some reason the city barriers were open. He would be lying to the woman he loved and just hoped he could make it sound convincing. His shoulders dropped and he thought of all the lies he would have to tell her from now on.

Dhazi's loathing for Calder was even stronger now, yet in spite of it all, Calder did seem to be a man of his word, but if it was going to go wrong, it would be now. He cruised to a stop just a few centimetres from the barrier and calmed himself.

"Exit permit!" snapped the guard as he reached out from his booth with one hand, with the other pointedly reaching for his weapon. Traffic stacked up behind as the man took his time to study the documents Dhazi offered.

"This is fake!" he snarled as he thrust the paperwork back. "You have committed a crime."

Dhazi knew that this was a game the guards liked to play to alleviate their boredom. They liked to see the anxiety on the drivers' faces and would string it out for as long as possible.

"It isn't, and I've broken no laws" he snapped. The guard's expression dropped, he scowled, wondering whether to carry on with the pretence, but decided against it as this young man didn't seem to be the type who was easily intimidated. "Identification!" he grunted.

Dhazi handed his ID over. "This isn't fake either."

The man snatched it out of his hand but said nothing as he scanned the barcode on the ID then checked the display on his terminal. Satisfied that it was correct, he scanned the barcode on the permit, then tossed the paperwork back at Dhazi as the barrier lifted.

Five hours later Dhazi was deep in the countryside heading towards the penal colonies. He'd never been this far out of the city before but had heard stories of the region. There was a ring of level ground five kilometres deep around the penal zone where no-one was allowed to live; there were no homes, no factories, no farms, animals or trees. A previous Calder had salted the ground, preventing any growth. It was about as barren as it could be. There was one road in and out. Nothing else.

There was an inner ring of trees that surrounded the colonies, dense woodland five kilometres deep that screened the various camps. The five camps were arranged in a circle, each one ten kilometres apart and graded for their level of security. Ayeka was in a grade two and was being moved to a grade three where the prison regime was much harsher.

Calder had assured him that everything was in place. He had also provided instructions on where to park when he got to the woods, and again, Dhazi had no choice but to believe him. He followed the directions along a track into woods, parked the car at the assigned spot then got out to make the two kilometre walk.

<<<<>>>

He made his way through the trees towards the remote location. The map reference showed he was just half a kilometre away and he had an hour before the transport was due to stop. He'd got over his initial shock of his life as it was going to be from now on, but it was laying heavy on his mind. Calder claimed that everything he did, everything he does and everything he is going to do is for the benefit of Matrea, to keep Matrea from collapsing into perpetual civil war. Dhazi found it hard to come to terms with, but all the sims had predicted it.

Every sim he had run that had Calder defeated, saw Matrea turn into a living hell with perpetual internecine warfare, and himself turning into a despotic ruler far worse than Calder. Once the factors surrounding Calder's descent into megalomania had been introduced, every sim showed ever increasing repression eventually leading to the complete disintegration of Matrean society. Of the thousands of sims that he had run, the only scenarios that showed any future for the people were the ones that maintained the status quo, with Calder maintaining his grip and Dhazi organising resistance to it. Dhazi just had to keep reminding himself that Calder's subjugation of the people, a repression that would continue to be harsh as it ever was, would be nothing compared to the alternatives.

He still wasn't sure if he trusted Calder, what if this was all some sort of elaborate trap and he *was* just a disposable pawn in Calder's plans. What if the deal he had made was phoney? If it was genuine, could he keep up the pretence? could he live with himself knowing that some of his friends would have to die?

He remembered Calder's words. *'they are not your friends, and you are not theirs'*. That had been easy for Calder to say, because he was used to ordering death. But could he keep it from Ayeka. He moved on, a sense of purpose filling him as he shook the thoughts from his head; they would cloud his judgement and he needed to concentrate if he was to save his girlfriend from the abuse.

Eventually the trees started to thin out and he saw a rough, under used road. On the other side of the road was a shack, one that had been used by forestry workers and abandoned when the prisons were built. According to Calder, this was where the rapes took place. He crossed the road and entered the shack. Inside there was a bed with a stained mattress and some rope.

He felt sick as he looked at it and imagined the horrors that the girls had endured. Killing the men would be much easier now, Ayeka was not going to be another one of their victims.

The gun case was under the bed. Inside was an assault rifle, complete with a telescopic sight, silencer and a box of ammunition. *'High velocity fragmentation, military use only, not for use by non-military organisations.'* These were the army's version of the ammunition the special security police used, far more powerful, far more deadly.

He recalled the training video that Calder had shown him, the instructional film on how to handle this weapon and the best tactics for its use. He had watched it and memorised everything, but all the while thinking of his friends who had seen it. In the last year at school, army recruitment officers had made weekly visits, encouraging students to sign up, painting service as a better life and an honour to be joining the massively bloated military that served Calder. Many believed it, and maybe it was true, but it was not how Dhazi had seen it at the time, and he still didn't. Those who signed up told themselves that it was preferable to a lifetime of grind in one of the factories, and maybe that was also true.

He checked his watch, he now had about twenty minutes. Loading the magazine and assembling the weapon took five; he went outside and shot at a tree. The silencer was effective, a sharp crack rather than a loud bang, though the recoil knocked him back on his feet. It was a bit harder than he had anticipated, but at least he now knew what to expect and could compensate for it. But he didn't know how this was going to pan out. There were going be two targets that would be moving, possibly in different directions. He needed to practice shots in quick succession and on targets that might be a distance apart. He took aim again, fired one shot then quickly took aim and shot at another tree. He continued shooting until he was confident that he could make the kill shots.

He went to the trees to check the damage. It was immense, with huge chunks torn away. He tried not to think about the effect that the bullets would have on a human body and hoped his kills would be clean and quick. He wondered what his life might have been if he had signed up to the military. Given his handling of the weapon and his accuracy, he may have been a sniper, taking lives at a distance. He would not have engaged the enemy in close combat to see the face of his enemy as they died at hands. But now he had done that, he had shot people and seen the sudden look of fear in their eyes and pain on their faces. Though that was in the heat of battle while breaking into the palace and he had seen it as necessary for self-defence. This would be different, this would be killing in cold blood, but he'd done that before as well.

Though whether or not to kill these two loathsome men was not an option, he had to do it to save Ayeka. She was tough and fearless, except for one thing, the thought of being raped terrified her, and she had always said that she would rather die than get in a situation where she could be sexually abused, and he believed her. She would try to get away, and they would shoot her.

From the tyre marks on the ground he could see where they always parked. So he crossed to the other side of the road, got in the shallow ditch and positioned himself appropriately.

"Five minutes," he muttered as the first beads of sweat formed on his brow. His heart began to thump in his chest, but he remembered the training video and breathed deeply, emptying his mind of all other thoughts and focussing completely on the view through the 'scope.

He heard it, the deep rumble of a diesel engine. He recognised it as the sound of a prison van, he'd heard the sound many times before when they passed through the streets having arrested people for whatever reason had been dreamt up that day.

Saekki and Kai aal were laughing and joking, both getting excited at the thought of what they could do to the girl they thought was helpless, both descending into ever more perverted fantasies. Kai-aal was driving, Saekki held two strips of paper in his hand, one shorter than the other. He held his hand out and Kai-aal took one, it was the short one.

"Hah," grunted Saekki "I get to go first for once."

"Just don't squash her, fatso," laughed Kai-aal as he reached over and slapped Saekki's fat belly.

In their arrogance, they had only put handcuffs on her and assumed that she would be like all the other girls were, timid and compliant. Little did they know that she had slipped out of the handcuffs by spitting on her skin and easing the restraints over. The metal had torn the skin from her knuckles, but she didn't care, she had heard the rumours about these two and had felt the change in the road surface, realising that they had turned off the main road. And she knew there was only one reason why they would do that. She would not cower down or beg, she would not try to lessen the abuse by being passive, she would fight like she had never fought before.

Saekki banged on the bulkhead.

"We're going to stop in a minute, and you're going to make us happy," he yelled, then burst out laughing.

Dhazi's heart pounded as he saw the van come into view. He was certain that they would not be able to see him, they would not even be looking for anyone. As he guessed from the tyre marks, the van pulled up outside the shack with its back towards him; he flicked the safety off and took aim at one of the doors.

"You get her ready, I'm going to take a leak," grunted Kai-aal. Both men got out and by chance, Dhazi was lined up on the driver's side. Kai-aal went to a nearby tree and started to relive himself, his back towards Dhazi.

The bullet struck a third of the way down the man's back and just to the left of his spine, fragmenting into shards, ripping through his body and blasting flesh, blood and bone out of his chest. The force slammed him up against the tree; he died without making a sound. Dhazi quickly adjusted his aim, the other man wasn't aware of what had happened and was almost at the back door of the van. Dhazi had no idea where Ayeka would be, and he couldn't risk a shot once the door was open or he might hit her. The man was now side on and presented a much smaller target. Dhazi shot anyway, though his aim was not so good this time and he hit low, the bullet striking Saekki's hip, destroying it. Saekki cried out as he crashed to the ground. Dhazi had no clear shot and got up and ran to the man to finish him off.

Ayeka heard the man cry out again but was confused as to what was happening. Expecting the door to open at any moment, she positioned herself. Outside, Dhazi levelled the gun at the man, making ready to pull the trigger.

"Please, I have children, a son your age," the man gasped, holding out his hand defensively. Dhazi paused, then saw Saekki's other hand fumbling for his weapon. Two shots to the chest silenced the man.

He opened the van door, quickly ducking back to avoid Ayeka's kick that had her foot grazing his chin.

"Dhazi!" she gasped, then she saw Saekki's body. "Where's the other one?"

"Dead."

"How did you know where I…"

"It's a long story, I'll tell you later, we've got to go." He hadn't banked on her asking this so soon and needed to delay answering to give him time to think of something convincing.

She looked down at the dead men, then went to get

TG TROUPER

their guns.

He stopped her. "No, we've got to leave them."

She looked at him, puzzled. "But they'll be useful to us."

"I know, but if we're found with them, they won't bother arresting us, they'll just kill us. There's a pond nearby, I'll dump my gun in there. We've got to go right now. We've got to get as far away as we can, because as soon as it's noticed that these two are late, a team will be sent out to look for them. I've got a car in the wood. Come on."

He grabbed her hand as they started to run, the hand that he had thought he would never hold again. But the joy he felt was tinged with guilt, the guilt he would feel every time he lied to her. Because he had to lie, there was no way he could ever tell her the truth; he was Calder's accomplice now and he hated himself for it.

Ayeka's relief at being rescued was tinged with confusion. She had known what was going to happen as soon as she felt the vehicle move off a smooth road onto a rougher one. She had actually known from the moment the two men took her and put her in the back of the vehicle. They had a look, a leering lustful look. They hadn't groped her, as they knew that they were being watched, and despite everything, blatant abuse of female prisoners by guards was forbidden and punishable. Abuse would come later, when there was no-one else around, that was obvious.

She'd heard rumours of an attack on the palace and

that a prisoner had been taken. Guards were muttering about the rebel leader being questioned, but the person had escaped, killing two guards in the process and she realised that it had to be Dhazi. No-one had ever escaped from the palace before, so how did he get away, and how did he know where she would be? These questions would be for later, right now they had to get as far away as possible.

Dhazi led her through the woods, some parts of which were dense and heavy going. An hour later they arrived at the car, exhausted. Only then did they embrace.

"I thought you were dead," he gasped.

"Calder's men were waiting for me, Lutcher had sold us out."

"No," he sighed as he remembered Hyodo's cruel betrayal.

Ayeka's emotions did not let her fully comprehend what he said. "Hyodo had a bad feeling and was trying to stop me from going."

"It wasn't Lutcher."

Again, what he said didn't register with her.

"Lutcher can't be trusted, we have to warn Orlo."

Dhazi broke away from her. "Ayeka, it wasn't Lutcher, it couldn't have been. I hadn't told him where the safe house was."

A look of confusion broke on her face. "But how…"

"We're not safe here, we've got to go. I'll tell you on the way. But first you've got to get out of the prison uniform. I was able to get some of your stuff from the house."

Ayeka quickly changed out of the uniform, dumping it at the side of the road and put on the clothes that he had brought. There was a brief moment when she was in her underware, but he couldn't look at her the way he used to. He couldn't admire the body of this beautiful young woman who had chosen him. He knew that intimacy was going to be a problem from now on because of the lies he was going to have to tell her, every day.

They got in the car and pulled away, with Dhazi driving much slower than she expected.

"Hurry, you said it's not safe."

"I don't want to draw any attention to us. Once they realise your transport is overdue, they'll send a squad to look for it, and I don't know what direction they'll come from."

"How did you know I was being transported? How did you know they would stop there? Where did you get the gun?"

"All in good time, let's just get away from here."

They did need to get away, but also he needed to give himself time to think of credible answers to any question she might ask. Seeing her again and holding her hand had done something to him. He loved her more than ever now, but forevermore he would have a demon on his shoulder telling him to lie to her, reminding him of what would happen if he didn't do what Calder wanted. He would be creating false friendships with people he knew he would send to their deaths, and the demon would laugh in his ear every time they took an action that saw a compatriot killed. Dhazi had demanded she be protected, and believed Calder when he said she would be, he had said that whatever happened she would not be harmed. He glanced at her, his heart fluttering as he thought of how much she meant to him, but how many deaths was she worth? He asked himself.

"All of them." he muttered quietly, but without meaning to.

"What did you say?"

"It's been hard without you..." he choked on his words as emotion got to him, he wiped a tear from his eye. "I love you so much, you are everything to me; the future will be hard for us now, but I will make sure you are safe." He would explain it all to her, but he would need to be careful, Ayeka's female intuition was razor sharp.

Two hours after leaving the site of Dhazi's ambush they had crossed the barren ring and were parked in a gateway to a field.

Dhazi put his arms over the steering wheel and rested his head on them, breathing deeply to calm himself. "Hyodo betrayed us."

Ayeka's jaw dropped open a fraction. "No, he couldn't have done."

"It's true."

"He was caught and tried as a traitor. We had to watch it on TV in the prison, we had no choice, they forced us. I saw him get executed."

"He wasn't executed."

"How do you know this?"

"Calder told me himself. He wanted to taunt me, he was boasting about how easy it was to get information on us."

She scowled. "And you trust him?"

"Ayeka, please, I didn't want to believe it either, but Calder showed me a video feed. Hyodo's alive and living with his parents. They didn't die, the cremation was faked."

"Why would Hyodo do that?"

"Calder did a deal, Hyodo's parents got the medicine they needed and on condition that he provided information on our activities." He thumped the steering wheel in frustration and anger. "He had no choice."

Ayeka scowled. "I don't believe it, not Hyodo, he was like family."

Dhazi sighed, he hadn't wanted to believe it either. "Calder showed me the letter Hyodo had written to him, saying he'd do anything for Calder if it would save his parent's lives. I know his handwriting, the letter was genuine. Think about it Ayeka, after his parents had supposedly died, think about all the times he had said sorry, and how he was worried that he would let us down."

Ayeka thought through everything that had happened, the horror of it all suddenly dawned on her.

"Ayeka, think about when Ellie and the others were killed, he was the only one to get away. He was devastated, we put it down to shock, but they were the first ones to die as a result of his betrayal. He'd told Calder where the house was."

She looked at him, anguished and close to tears. "He knew Calder's men were waiting for me, he'd told them I'd be there, didn't he?"

"Yes."

"They grabbed me, stuck a needle in me and I don't remember anything after that. When I came to I was in prison." She paused and looked at him curiously. "You said you thought I was dead, how did you know I wasn't?"

"It was a cruel mind trick by Calder. Hyodo didn't see you being captured, all he saw was a soldier with a flame thrower, he thought they were just going to capture you, but Calder made him think that they'd burned you alive."

Ayeka was confused. "Why did he do that?"

"Hyodo had told Calder that I was the leader, and Calder needed us to attack the palace. He needed me to get in so he could make an example of me. Something that would send a message, *'you can try to overthrow me, but this is what will happen'*. But we weren't planning on attacking, were we? So he needed something to spur me on, and by making Hyodo believe he had led you to your death, he was devasted and all the more convincing for it.

"Calder said he knew we were going to attack. He had all the information on when the attack would take place because…" Dhazi's words faltered as he thought of what he was about to say. "…because Hyodo had bugged our room. You remember he replaced that socket? It was that. Calder heard everything."

Ayeka gagged and started to cry, putting her hands to her head, unable to comprehend the actions of a person she thought was a friend, someone she cared about, taken into their home. And all the time they were right next to the bug, feeding it intel. He'd made conversation with them both, knowing that it was all being listened to. Then she thought of the times that she and Dhazi had been alone in the room.

"Was it a…"

He had anticipated her question. "Just sound."

Ayeka flung open the door and doubled over to throw up. A moment later she pounded her fist on the dashboard

"No, no, no, no, no," she yelled.

Dhazi sighed, despite everything, there was a tiny bit of him that did understand why Hyodo went through with it although he could never forgive him. "Once you were taken and Calder knew the date of the attack, he released Hyodo from his obligation. His parents were cured, and he went to live with them. He still thinks you were burned alive."

"The trial was a sham, wasn't it?"

"Yes, he would have been arrested for something."

"The petrol bomb attack on the police car, do you think he meant to kill the cops?"

"I don't know. He *was* absolutely devastated; it's one thing to rat on your friends, and quite another to see your friends die as a result of your betrayal." Cold shot through his veins as he thought about what he had just said.

"Who did they execute?"

"Some guy, they'd dressed him in Hyodo's clothes, and the bag over the head? That'd never been done before. I should have noticed that, but I was so shocked that it didn't register. I believed it was Hyodo."

"And it made you even more determined to get Calder."

"Yes, if that's even possible. I went with your father to get the body that we both thought was you."

"Oh my god, Mum and Dad, they..."

"I spared your mother the details. I told your father though. Being told that you had been burned to death was too horrific, too ghastly and too much for him to comprehend. It didn't hit him until we were at the crematorium, he broke down. I haven't seen him since, so I don't know how he's doing."

"When I was in prison, they told me that I was a special category and that I wouldn't be allowed any visitors, ever. So you and my parents thought I was dead and had no way of knowing the truth."

"Correct, but because we thought it was you that had been killed by Calder's men, we couldn't go to the police, and obviously there couldn't be a proper funeral, so your Dad bribed someone at the crematorium. He said that they would say that you had moved away to live on your own."

"I've got to go and see them," she said firmly. He knew it would be pointless to even try to talk her out of it.

"Okay, but we've got to be careful, every regular cop, every riot cop and every special security operative will have our picture and will be on the lookout for us." He started the car and pulled away.

Military Police Squad.

Forty kilometres away a military police Captain was looking down at the bodies. A subordinate officer showed him a bag full of bullet shards.

"Military. They're the only ones that'll pass right through." He looked back at the bodies, then went to Kai-aal and studied the hole in the man's back.

"A single shot, well aimed," he muttered quietly, then went to Saekki and saw the three wounds. He looked over at the other side of the road then talked himself through the theory that was forming in his mind. "He waited there. The guy by the tree was shot first, then a shot to the hip put this one down, then the shooter came across and two at close range to the chest finished him off."

He thought about the talk surrounding these two men and grunted, well aware that the rumours were almost certainly true. "A squaddie did this, they probably raped his sister. Okay, find out if anyone is AWOL."

"You mean any more than usual?" scoffed his subordinate.

"Yeah, well, there's always that."

He looked back across the road, noticing the white of the trees where the bark had been stripped away. He went to them and saw the bullet fragments embedded in the wood. He looked back at the bodies, the dead men had no weapons that could fire these rounds, so a gun battle hadn't taken place. A few scenarios filled his head, but only one explained the damage to the trees.

"Why would a soldier need practice shots?" he muttered to himself, then dismissed his speculation. "Who was the prisoner?"

The subordinate read through the document on his data terminal. "The file says it was Ayeka Beka. She was suspected of arson attacks, and it says here that she was an uncooperative prisoner. It seems she was a bit of a handful, which was probably why she was being transferred to a higher security prison."

The Captain got in the back of the van and looked at the handcuffs, noticing that they hadn't been opened or cut off. He saw the blood and fragments of skin on the inside of the cuffs and the drops of blood on the floor. He realised what she had done, he had seen this tried before, but no-one had ever succeeded in getting them off. He was impressed but didn't show it.

He scoffed as he looked at the ankle cuffs that obviously hadn't been used. "If they had put those on her she'd have never got them off," he muttered with an undertone of irritation.

He called the subordinate over and talked through the scenario that he thought most likely. "My guess is that there was only one shooter, and whoever killed these men opened the door. She'd already freed herself, and if what I suspect is correct, then the shooter killed these men for revenge and set her free. The recovered bullet fragments are too small for us to get a definitive link to a specific weapon, the lab technician will be able to." He looked around, taking in the remoteness of the area. "There won't be any witnesses and I think it's unlikely that we'll ever find the shooter. Get Ayeka Beka's image circulated." He paused and thought for a bit. "Lethal force is authorised."

The subordinate didn't flinch when he heard this, even though everyone knew that this meant *'shoot first, don't bother asking questions'*.

<<<<>>>

There was silence for a while as they drove, with Ayeka struggling to process Hyodo's betrayal; it also gave time for Dhazi to think of what questions she would ask and come up with creditable answers to them. Eventually he had a plausible story. He pulled over to the side of the road, hating himself for what he had to do.

"When Hyodo told me what happened to you, I wanted to get Calder right away. I told Lutcher and Orlo what had taken place, or at least what I believed had taken place. Lutcher was beside himself with anger. I'd never realised how much you meant to him, he said he would have done anything to protect you, and I believe him."

Ayeka swallowed hard, she hadn't realised it either.

"Orlo was angry too, but he showed it in his own way. He seemed calm but I could tell he was seething inside. He urged caution, and he was right, we had to plan it carefully. They both taught me how to fight, and we made our plans sitting at the table."

"Where Calder could hear everything."

"Exactly. Calder knew everything, he knew that the attack was a diversion and that I was to make my way in alone. Lutcher had told me to think about you and how you died, again, at least how I thought you died. But they knew I was coming and yeah, I got captured. *'I'm not lying to her... yet'* he thought to himself as a sick feeling rose inside him.

"They tied me to a chair in a cell, then Calder came in and told me everything, he showed me Hyodo's note and showed me the video of him. Then he left and these other people came in." He looked away, he couldn't face her knowing what he had said was only partially true, but the rest would be complete lies. He showed her the puncture wounds on the backs of his hands and in the crooks of his elbows.

"They hooked me up to these bags of fluid, they said it was some sort of drug that would break my will. But I could see the door, it was my way out, and I focussed on that, saying to myself that I had to get out to save you. I said it over and over in my mind, it was the only thought I had. I was so fixated on getting out that the drugs didn't work, I heard someone say that my willpower was too great.

"I pretended to pass out. They said the drugs weren't working. So they pulled the tubes out and dragged me to a cell. That's when I heard about you being moved, the guards were joking about the two men and their no-so-secret shack. I remembered every detail.

"They didn't seem to know what to do with me. I felt for sure that I would be tried as a traitor and executed. I made out that the drugs had made me permanently drowsy, and I heard someone say that Calder now didn't want to do that as it would make me a martyr, so they were just going to keep me locked up."

"How were you able to escape?"

"I just got lucky. Before the attack, I recorded some of the police when they came to the restaurant, they said how the new palace guards were incompetent. A guard came into my cell with some food." Dhazi shrugged. "He'd brought a knife for me to eat it with, a sharp knife. I killed him with it, then made my way out. There was a guard by jetty, I killed him and got away." Dhazi supressed his sick feeling but couldn't control his shaking.

She reached over, stroking his arm to comfort him.

He closed his eyes and sighed. "Things are going to be difficult for us, the drugs work by creating a feeling of extreme guilt so people are willing to confess and to answer questions truthfully. They didn't work on me, well, not completely, they have affected me though, and I hope it's not permanent. I feel this massive burden, I feel responsible for the deaths of our friends."

Bile rose in his throat. Would she believe this crass excuse.

"All the deaths, they're on Hyodo, not you."

He took hold of her hand, forcing sincerity and hoping that she wouldn't see the hollow that was in his eyes.

"Ayeka, I need you to understand that events have changed me, and these drugs, well, I may not always be as rational as before, I may behave differently."

"It'll get better, I'll help you," she said in that soft reassuring voice that had always melted his heart. He looked at her, feeling her compassion for him and all the while the hate he felt for himself gnawed away at his soul.

She held him tight. "You're still the man I love and knowing the risks you took to rescue me makes me love you even more."

He swallowed hard, unable to stop his tears, but he knew he'd said enough and was sure that she didn't suspect anything. Though her words, so soft and so comforting in any other situation, cut him like a knife now.

She pulled away and wiped the tears from his face. "We need to go."

Roadblock.

"Oh no," she gasped. "Dhazi, there's a roadblock."

"I see it." He glanced in the rear view mirror. "There's a police vehicle behind us." He quickly scanned the road ahead. "There are no turnings off and we can't turn around."

"Dhazi, what are we going to do?"

He thought quickly; Calder had promised that she would be protected, and he hoped beyond hope that the man would keep to his word, so whatever happened, she should be safe.

"We have no choice, we have to stop or they'll shoot us."

The car coasted to a stop ten metres from a barrier. Men stepped in front and aimed their weapons at them, others went to the side and did the same. Behind them the police car stopped, and more men got out, again, with weapons drawn and aimed.

"Get out and put your hands up!" yelled an officer.

Ayeka hesitated, she looked at Dhazi and swallowed hard. "Remember, whatever happens, I love you."

"Get out now!" screamed the officer. "Get out or we will open fire."

The two got out and raised their hands.

"Get on your knees and keep your hands up."

An officer walked towards her, a scanner in his hand. "Keep still and keep your eyes open," he snarled.

She couldn't help blinking as the dazzling beam scanned down her face.

"I said keep your eyes open," he shouted. He scanned her face again, this time she managed to comply with his orders.

He grunted as he read the file that was displayed. "Is your name Ayeka Beka?" he demanded.

"Yes," she replied and braced herself for rough treatment.

"It says here that you're a law-abiding citizen. I suggest you keep it that way," he snarled, then went to scan Dhazi.

"Leave him," came the voice of his commander. "It's a girl we're looking for." The man, irritated that he wouldn't have the kudos in being the first to spot the fugitive, grunted and pointed to the two of them.

"Get in the car and clear off."

Dhazi and Ayeka wasted no time in getting in the car. The barrier raised and they drove away.

"What was that all about? I felt sure we were going to be shot," she gasped. Dhazi suspected that this was Calder's work and that he was sticking to his word to protect her. "They must have entered your details wrong when you were taken to prison," was the best explanation he could come up with.

A few hours earlier Calder had seen the report of Ayeka's escape, the killings and the arrest authorisation issued by the Captain. "Well done, Dhazi," he muttered. "But without her, you will never reach your full potential." He entered a code and pressed 'Replace'. This code enabled all police and prison records along with any backup files relating to her to be altered and the name changed. In an instant, Ayeka Beka had gone from being a prisoner on the run to be shot on sight, to a law abiding civilian. He called up her name in the population database and entered a 'P' in a special column. This meant she was protected from any harassment. Only six other people had this, Dhazi, his parents, Hyodo and his parents.

"Are you going to tell Lutcher and Orlo about Hyodo betraying us?"

"No, if I do they'll go looking for him, and it might cause a split if they know that someone so close to us was a traitor, and we have to stay together as one."

"So, what will you say to them?"

"I won't say anything. I'll let them believe what everyone believes: Hyodo was caught, tried for treason and executed."

Ayeka thought for a moment, shaking her head slightly. "I'm not happy about keeping secrets from our allies."

Frustration was starting to get to him, from the enormous secret that he would have to keep from her and the lies he had told her, and he almost lost his temper.

"I don't like it either, but what are we supposed to do?" he snapped, then instantly apologised. "I'm sorry, it's just the stress of all this has finally got to me. I held it in, I had to be strong, and it was hard without you. It was so hard believing you were dead." He put his head in his hands. "It's not lying, it's withholding the truth. There's a difference. There are some things that can't be shared, things that nobody else can ever know about, no matter how bad the situation, otherwise things can end up worse."

She sensed his distress and put her hand on his arm to comfort him. "It's okay, I understand. There are some secrets that no-one else should know."

'No Ayeka, you don't understand, you will never understand. You must never know what I have agreed to,' said the voice in his head.

"What do we do now, Dhazi?"

He raised his head as proudly as his hollow soul would allow. "We continue the fight against Calder, we carry on."

Author's note:

Hyodo is a Korean word that means absolute devotion to one's parents and to care for them until they die.

Other works by TG Trouper

Astrid book 1: War changes people.

Astrid book 2: Good people do bad things.

Astrid book 3: The early missions.

Perfect Strangers.

The Story – Be careful what you read.

Published by Austin Macauley in paperback and eBook format. Available worldwide and can be ordered from any bookshop or online vendors or by scanning this QR code.

tgtrouper@gmail.com

Printed in Great Britain
by Amazon

62958115R00167